BENEATH THE MASK

BENEATH

THE GRASSLAND TRILOGY

THE MASK

DAVID WARD

AMULET BOOKS

NEW YORK

The Library of Congress has catalogued the hardcover edition of this book as follows:

Ward, David, 1967–
Beneath the mask / David Ward.
p. cm. — (The grassland trilogy; bk. 2)
Summary: After tasting freedom, the former slaves are soon back under the control of the menacing Spears, and this time Corki and Pippa are separated as Corki, in training to be a Spear, seeks a way to work within the system to gain freedom for himself and his friends.
ISBN 978-0-8109-7074-8 (harry n. abrams : alk. paper)
[1. Slavery—Fiction. 2. Torture—Fiction. 3. Science fiction.] I. Title.
PZ7.W1873Ben 2008
[Fic]—dc22
2007049836

Paperback ISBN 978-0-8109-5449-6

Text copyright © 2003 David Ward
First published by Scholastic Canada Ltd.
Published in hardcover by Amulet Books in 2008
Map by Paul Heersink/Paperglyphs

Book design by Chad W. Beckerman

Printed and bound in U.S.A.
10 9 8 7 6 5 4 3 2 1

ABRAMS
THE ART OF BOOKS SINCE 1949

115 West 18th Street
New York, NY 10011
www.abramsbooks.com

For my parents,
Bev and Pat Ward

Special thanks to adult readers
Christianne Hayward,
Mark Rankin, and Mark Mason
Ward; and to student readers
Vignan, Allen, Casey, and Shahin.
Thank you, guys!

I would also like to thank Sandy
Bogart Johnston; Tracy Zuber; my
agent, Scott Treimel; and the most
capable team at Amulet.

I am grateful to the B.C. Arts
Council for their support
of this novel.

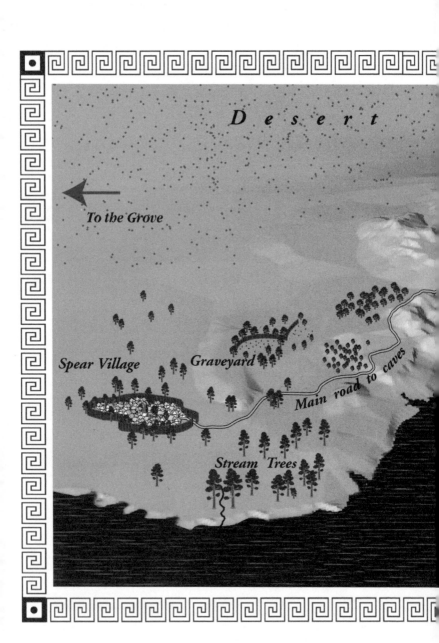

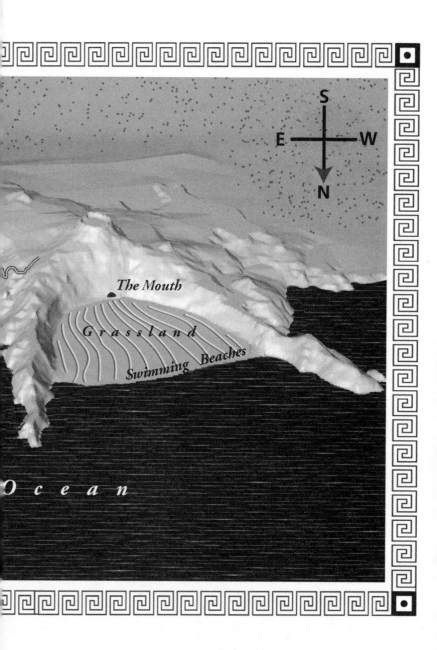

BENEATH THE MASK

PART ONE

I

IF WE REMAINED QUIET, THERE was a chance some of us could make it to the ship alive.

Pippa squirmed beside me. "Ashes," she mumbled. "Ashes and fire." She tried to sit up but I pushed her back down until she stopped moving. It did not stop her words from sounding again in my head.

Ashes and fire. It was a recurring dream for her— even more so as the day of our escape drew closer. I glanced above the high grass, where the rest of the former cellmates lay within touching distance. Some rested, others watched the thicker woods behind us. Against the night sky their gray cloaks and hoods flickered occasionally, like the tree shadows so near.

Ahead, drifting in swirls of mist, the outline of a ship swayed against the stars. A brilliant moon, close to full, shone down on our scattered hiding places. Its face played a deadly game with me, lighting up anything that showed itself while making the shadows still deeper. "Ashes and fire," she whispered again.

"Be quiet, Pippa," I hissed.

I pulled my gaze away from the rustling in the woods to look at her. The woman clothing she had taken from the Spear village sat so loosely on her small shoulders, it rustled with the lifting of a finger. I wished again that she had settled for her old work-cloth as I had. Careful not to look at her eyes, I eased my hand away from her.

Her lips tightened. "Corki, if I stood up right now and screamed, it might be no different than what could happen to us later. You *must* listen to me. And Tia must as well."

I risked a more thorough glance behind, above the short bramble against our backs. Dark trees rose at the foot of the mountain. Its enormous shadow crept all the way to the ocean, and one arm of it, a giant wall of stone to our left, stretched into the sea, blocking our view of the bay. It also hid our secret, the very reason why we lay still as stones, waiting for the morning.

"Do you want *them* to find us?" I hissed at Pippa. "Do you know what they will do?"

She nodded. "Yes, I know. But I would rather face Strays than something I do not know. They were Diggers once. Just like us."

"But now they are *not* like us," I growled. "They steal our food and attack at night. This is why we fixed the Spear ship. It is why we are lying here—to escape from them!" Before I could say more, the grasses rustled at my side and a strong hand gripped the back of my hair.

A long shadow moved across our faces. Tia had crept up without me sensing her. "No more talk!" Her dark eyes flashed and her face hardened.

"Tia, listen to me," Pippa whispered. "You must—"

Tia's hand left my braid in a blur and struck Pippa sharply on the forehead, with almost no sound. No one had hit my cellmate before without me striking back. I never imagined Tia being the first to do it.

"Forgive me!" she whispered urgently. "Forgive me.

But you *must* be silent. The Strays are so close. And we are almost away." She caught sight of my raised fist and tears of desperation welled up. "I beg you, be silent. How many have we already lost tonight? Shall I lose you both as well?"

Although Pippa's shoulders shook, she did not speak or cry out. Instead she nodded, pressed my hand down, then pushed her face miserably into the grass.

Tia slumped in relief. She reached out and stroked Pippa's hair gently, then risked a few words to me. "Come. Thief is waiting near the beach. Bran can stay with Pippa."

Until that moment I had not realized that her brother lay hidden half a stone's throw ahead of us and closer to the sand. He nodded at me. I smiled, hoping he could see. No one was as fearful as Bran, but other than Thief, or maybe Tia, I could not think of anyone who had more courage. It felt good to see him. All night he had worked beside me, keeping the others quiet and carrying more than his share through the tangled woods. Tia signed for him to join us.

A crackle of branches a moment later made all of us

cling to the earth. Bran's head went down. There were no voices, only the slapping of brush against bare skin as the Strays made their way through the undergrowth. It was difficult to tell exactly how many there were, for more sounds were beginning to mingle as they searched closer toward the beach.

The white undersides of leaves glimmered here and there as the Strays pushed them aside. I felt for a stone, easing it gently from beneath the roots of the tall grasses. Above their tips I thought I could see the flash of eyes. In the dim light, flesh and bone seemed little different from trunk and branch with the wind blowing the forest into life.

When the crashing started again I squeezed Pippa's hand so hard she pulled away. I turned the stone around in my palm to get the best grip. I would aim for the head, one shot only—eyes or nose were best. Bran would have to move closer to take the Strays at the back. I signed *Come*. Beside me, Tia had risen to a crouch, ready to spring at our attackers. I slid to my knees, shoulder to shoulder now between Bran and Tia. Beads of sweat glistened on the backs of her hands.

Ten strides away another crashing broke out to our left. I raised my throwing arm. Tia caught my wrist. She shook her head and I peered into the darkness. It was a Digger this time, one of us, unable to contain his fear any longer. I could hear his sobbing as he ran back into the woods. It was a desperate try for escape, but I understood it. The Strays burst forward immediately to start the chase. The woods erupted with shouts.

We sat upright, four of us, waiting for attackers to break through the grass. Again I raised my arm, ready to strike the first head that showed itself. This close to the chase, I was able to distinguish many footfalls as Stray after Stray landed on a patch of hard soil just strides from our noses. The smell of their unwashed bodies wafted toward us.

We could hear them pushing one another forward, spurring the ones in front to move faster, closer to the hunt. Tia stifled a scream when one of them tripped and a foot slid through the grass, crashing into my knee. As my hand started down toward it, Pippa caught my wrist. The toes crinkled against my skin. Then the foot pushed off to stumble after the other Strays.

Only our eyes moved until the noise gradually lessened

and the Strays followed their prey back toward the stream-trees. Tia's forehead came to rest against my shoulder. I could feel her sigh on my arm. Pippa was still holding my hand, my rock frozen in the air. My own breath was coming in gasps.

"Let's go," Tia whispered a moment later.

I looked to Pippa, uncertain whether I should be angry or thankful for her silence. I suddenly longed for the peace of our cell, where I could speak to her in quiet. "What should I do?"

She did not answer at first. Her eyes, normally so green in the sun, stared back colorless in the dim. "This is all wrong, Corki. But do what you must to help the others. I will wait with Bran." She touched my face. "Only do not be caught. I will not live without you. That much you know."

"I will not be caught."

It hurt like a shell cut to leave her, even for only a short while. There was some comfort entrusting her to Bran, especially with the Strays off hunting for the moment. At least, that is what I told myself as I hunched lower to follow Tia.

Bran gave me a nervous grin from under his hood as we squirmed past him. I pressed my stone into his hand.

"Run toward the ship if you hear *anything*," I whispered. He nodded.

I followed Tia's heels closely, no longer with the freedom to stand or even crouch. There was less cover away from the trees. Any Strays looking this way from the beach would quickly see us in the moonlight.

The grasses, so close to my nose, drowned out the scent of the woods behind us. They were not as tall here as the grasses in our bay, where shards lay hidden under deep roots. This grass was soft and green in the daylight, like the leaves of trees.

The other Diggers stared as we crawled past, their arms wrapped tightly around their bundles—for both warmth and comfort. I hardly recognized any of them, crouched as they were in the grass. Most were wearing gray work-cloths, although here and there I caught sight of color against the pale grass. For the first time in our lives we had things we could call our own. Warm wraps, a comb, even a necklace or two of glittering stones. Some of the Onesies had taken as much as they could carry from our weeks spent in the Spear village. Now it only slowed them down. I wondered briefly how many of them had considered joining the Strays before this night.

When I suddenly felt sand mixed in among the roots, I crawled faster to catch up with Tia. She stopped, then nodded. A flicker of movement caught my eye. Whether it was a sweep of an arm or a twirl of sand flung up by the wind I could not tell. Had we passed all the Diggers who were with us?

Tia lifted an open palm: *Peace.*

Despite her assurance, my fingers trembled as I raised myself a hand-span to look.

A lone figure lay sprawled as we were, his feet at our faces and his arms pressed to the ground. The crash of the ocean was louder here and the light noticeably brighter. Tia and I made our way up either side of him, so close I could have smelled his breath if the wind were not blowing.

Turning, he raised his palm against the sky and signed *Peace.* I could barely make out the jagged scar running along the inside of his wrist, but I knew it was there. I had been with him when it happened.

"Thief," Tia whispered. "Anything?"

I could feel the rumble of his chuckle. Only Thief would laugh at a time like this. Although his black eyes were hard to see, his teeth flashed brightly. When he spoke, his accent rose only enough to be heard above the wind.

"No Strays." He pointed toward the ship.

I looked out. From where we lay the beach stretched in front of us like the belly of a long gray snake playing with the lapping water. Other than that, there was not a hint of movement between the mountain headlands in either direction, except for the pounding surf. For a brief moment my hopes rose.

"They are out there," Tia muttered. "Everywhere. I can smell them."

I leaned even closer to Thief. The Strays had a distinct odor from living among the burned and dead things of the Spear village. It announced them long before they could be seen. Ash was thick among the burned dwellings too, and its whiteness made the Strays look all the more frightening by day, and terrifying at night. In the last few days their raids on our food had become more dangerous than before.

They attacked at night in groups of no fewer than

twenty and carried stones or pointed sticks. Their eyes would flare in our firelight and their shadows seemed to haunt the trees. Now the daylight had become just as dangerous. Too dangerous to remain.

I spat downwind.

Thief grunted. He shared my feelings. The Strays were traitors, Diggers turned wild who had left us soon after we were out of Grassland. I could still remember them clinging to Tia while we searched the broken houses of the Spear village for food. But when we had gathered enough to eat they began to wander off, greedy to find any of the Spear things that remained after the fires started by Outside had burned the houses to the ground. Strays did not want to share as Pippa taught us to. Instead they had peered at us through broken doorways and smoking walls, waiting for the right moment to steal.

When we had moved to the stream-trees, they followed at a distance, under the cover of the leaves and the dark, to find where we would store our food. As more of our company left, the Strays gained in strength and numbers. Although they had no Threesie as we did, a leader rose up among them, one who was jealous of the food we gathered from the trees or the shore of Grassland. In the end, we decided to escape by boat, using one of the Spear ships still docked in the bay. It had taken a long time to repair that ship, working late at night and as silently as possible. But there was little choice. It was our only chance.

Tia's voice broke into my thoughts. "It is time," she was saying. "We will get everyone on board, then wait for dawn. As soon as we can see enough to get safely out of the bay without crashing into the rock"—she fixed her gaze on both of us in turn—"we go."

Even looking at her gave me more strength. Tia was the only Threesie I had ever known. She was strong, and thought faster than the rest of us. The little Onesies clung to her every word. Even at twelve summers and an experienced Digger, I found myself relying on her wisdom to finally get away from Grassland.

I smiled at Thief and made the sign for *Go*. He slapped the sand excitedly and was already on his way back to the others before I had turned fully around to follow him.

Bran moved aside when I reached him. "There has been no further sound," he whispered. "I think they are gone."

"Pippa," I said, brushing away a strand of her golden hair.

"I am ready," she whispered.

I leaned my forehead against hers. "All is well, Pippa. The Strays have gone back to look for us near the stream-trees. We will be away soon." I allowed myself a brief moment of happiness. "Think of it! We have not been Separated, and no Spears or Strays can stop us!"

She smiled weakly, her eyes gazing over my shoulder. She kissed my cheek and I felt a warm tingle flow through me.

After crouching low to the ground for so long, it was frightening to stand and lift our burdens into the moonlight. The earth had seemed so comforting, and by ducking down we could disappear in the tall grass. Now my heart pounded. I kept waiting for the bite of a stone or stick in my back.

At Tia's signal, Diggers rose out of the grasses from where they had hidden and formed a ragged line behind her. Pippa did not speak as we pushed through the grasses, but she let me hold her hand without resisting. If she was annoyed with me for choosing Tia's way, she did not show it. Several times she stopped to help some of the Onesies gather their things.

"Have you been praying?" I whispered.

She nodded. "I have not stopped."

"Good."

There was no more hiding now. Our only chance was to get on board our ship before we were discovered. At the water's edge we stopped. We had agreed to swim to the ship with as few burdens as possible. Most cellmates carried their bundles in baskets, or wrapped in cloth taken from the Spear village.

While we waited for those in front to enter the water, I stared nervously back at the mountain. It was foolish, I knew, but I could not help imagining the slopes crawling with Spears. I shook my head. The Strays were our only concern now.

"Hurry up, hurry up," I muttered.

Pippa leaned against me. "I will miss the stream-trees," she whispered.

Water swirled at my ankles. The cool splash on my legs felt colder than our afternoon swims. I would miss those the most. A rogue wave crashed into me, and the spray off my shins reached as high as my chin. I frowned. It reminded me of the cold seawater the Spears sent through the Onesie cages for the First Cleansing, the night they brought new Diggers into the cells. I wiped the water droplets from my chin. There were some things it was better not to remember.

My hands clenched and my eyes flickered back to the mountain. I hated the Spears. The very thought of those tall figures with their frowning masks and long black capes chilled me more than the water. Pippa had somehow found forgiveness for them, but I never would.

I shook my head. We go to a better place, I told myself. I turned my back on Grassland and faced the sea.

Pippa remained staring at the mountain. "We do not even know where we are going," she said. When I did not answer, she shivered, then faced the water too. "It is cold." Gentle waves broke on the shore, only to return to tug at our legs. She squeezed my fingers. "At least your hand is warm."

Other Grasslanders were whispering as well. For the first time since we had left the fireside at the stream-trees there were nervous giggles and soft laughter. Hurrying up to us, with their bundles perched on the tops of their heads, Thief and Feelah waved. Her thick braids seemed to stick out everywhere despite Pippa's attempts to keep them controlled.

"Slow down, Coriko," she said with a grin. She took hold of Pippa's other hand, and I was forced to manage two bundles under one arm. The four of us went forward. It would be easier now with Feelah so close. She could speak the language of some of the others, and they would understand without having to sign. I could see Tia chest-deep in the water. She was quietly urging the others past and warning them to silence.

"They should be more quiet," I whispered ahead to Bran. "It is still dangerous." My feet searched for firm footholds between the rocks and sand.

"Yes, it is," he said solemnly, glancing back. His determined chin stuck out from his hood, reminding me a little of Tia. As we splashed up to his sister, pushing our bundles ahead of us, she gave a quick smile of encouragement. Her arm rested on a long rope that broke the water near her shoulder and led all the way up to the nose of the ship.

All is well, she signed. I was about to return the sign when her eyes suddenly flicked over my shoulder and her hands froze on the rope. I turned to face the beach, letting my bundle float free.

"Strays."

2

THE SAND WAS COVERED WITH them. Some were running from the trees nearest the mountain. Others stood motionless at the water's edge only thirty strides away. Everywhere I looked, glinting white arms, faces, and chests appeared to float above the water like the skeletons of some fleshless creatures. Many of the Strays were holding pointed throwing sticks above their heads, which from this far away looked more like giant horns than pieces of wood.

For the briefest moment I wondered if the bones of the dead Spears had come to life. Seeing a horde of them all together made my teeth chatter.

Their leader was among them. He stood taller than the others, and the Strays ran in front of him like animals.

Staring at them made me realize just how many they had become.

Tia was the first to awaken from our fear. She pushed off from the rope. "Swim! All of you. Get to the ship!"

At the sound of her voice the leader of the skeletons raised his throwing stick. I gritted my teeth, waiting for the roar and charge as the wild figures surged into the water.

"Move, Pippa! Swim!" Pulling hard on my cellmate's hand I forced her ahead of me and into the pack of escaping Diggers. Someone's splash shot up my nose, burning the back of my throat.

"Corki," Pippa panted. "There are so many."

We thrashed forward into deeper water, where our feet could no longer touch the sand. And then all the badness happened at once.

The Strays started throwing stones. Big ones.

Like a rain of fist-size drops, stones began to tear holes in the water directly in front of us. Bran cried out, and from the corner of my eye I saw a stone glance off the side of his head. He went under. With a gasp I tried to raise myself higher in order to protect Pippa.

Something struck my back so hard, the air wheezed

out of my body, as if I were trying to blow embers into a blaze. Grasping for Pippa, I went under. Her fingers tore loose as I sank deeper into the murk. From somewhere above I could hear her muffled screaming.

Someone's foot kicked the side of my head as they swam for the ship. I could feel my lungs on fire and I knew I was only a breath away from sucking in as much water as my lungs could take. But as the salty ocean flowed into my mouth a new pain yanked me back into the open air.

"*Coreeko!*" Thief's voice rang in my ear as I coughed and sputtered. His fingers gripped my hair as if he meant to fling me to the stars. Feelah's big nose pushed into my face, and I felt her hands lifting me up from underneath.

"Coreeko, swim!" she yelled in my ear. Still dizzy, I reached out to start a feeble paddle. Stones continued to plunge into the sea, but I hardly noticed. I only wanted to stay afloat.

Then another arm slipped under my chest. "Here, Corki," Pippa said, "swim with me."

Although my back throbbed, more air than water was getting inside my lungs. I could feel my strength coming back. The waves churned with swimming Diggers and sea spray coming from every direction. I could not tell where the ship was.

Tia's voice rang out. "Where is Bran?" She looked about helplessly at the floundering Diggers. "Feelah," she called, "is he near you?"

Feelah swung her shaggy head. "No. Poor Bran." She waved behind us.

"I am going back!" Tia yelled.

"Wait!" I croaked. Thief let go of my head. I began to tread water to look back for Bran, expecting to see white-flecked foam and the spray of a hundred Strays charging into the water. But they were not attacking. They stood silent at the water's edge like a forest of young trees.

"Can you see him, Pippa?" Tia's voice was rising to a shriek.

My head was beginning to clear. I had seen Bran get hit, so he must be near.

"Peace, Tia!" I made quiet swirls of water with my hands so that I could hear better. The sound of sand and small stones scraping off the beach with each returning wave filled my ears. Yet in between the surges was a silence, louder than the ocean. It brought a wave of hatred across the water strong enough to make me choke.

Thief raised a closed fist and shook it. *Death.*

My own hand started to rise, but Pippa reached out. "Don't, Corki. Let us find Bran with the strength we have left."

I spat as far as I could toward the beach. Against the blackness of the woods behind him, the ash-white arm of the Strays' leader rose once more into the air. The rattle of a hundred pointed sticks reached us before we could take a single stroke in search of Bran.

"Under!" I yelled. "Feelah, tell everyone to go under! Breathe!"

She nodded and we dove, cutting off the sound of Feelah's words as the water rose above our heads. Moments later the sticks began to land, slashing through the murk like a storm of shooting stars. Pippa tried to pull us deeper, hoping beyond hope that none of the sticks would find its mark.

When we came back up, many Diggers were already closer to the ship. The sticks continued to fall. I looked wildly again for Bran and caught sight of Tia, beginning to head back into the rain of spears. "No, Tia!"

Pippa popped up beside me and together we reached out, caught Tia's work-cloth, and pulled her back. She sobbed as we swam, struggling to break free, until a pointed stick cut through the hood of her work-cloth. Then she kicked out strongly for the ship. I let go of her. My strength was almost gone, and from the sloppy strokes of Pippa beside me, I knew that she did not have much strength left either.

The blackened sides of the ship gleamed in the moonlight as we approached, and the crossbeams of the mast stretched crookedly heavenward like a tree struck by lightning. Pippa had once pointed out such a tree near the village.

"I cannot last much longer, Corki," she puffed beside me.

I was so tired I could not answer. As I reached for the rope ladder hanging from the railing far above, I glanced back to the beach. Diggers continued to swim up to the ship, and I strained to see if there was any sign of Bran among them. I tightened my grip on the rope and watched Tia's tall form slip over the railing above.

When my feet finally hit the deck, I fell to my knees beside a weeping Tia.

"He may still come," I panted, then rolled onto my back. "He may still come."

Diggers were sprawled all over the deck, most gasping, some crying. The ship swayed peacefully, and it seemed impossible that only a moment ago we had been in the madness of escape.

I crawled over to Pippa on my hands and knees, feeling the pains of my wounds afresh. Thief stared out over the railing. There was a quiet between us, and I knew that Bran's face was in his thoughts as much as my own.

"The Strays are not coming," Feelah whispered beside him. "Just standing there."

I peeked over the side. A swath of moonlight lit the ash-white bodies brightly. They had not moved, but stood swaying like a ghostly army about to face an enemy from the sea.

"No sense," I whispered.

I wanted Tia to be with us, to stare out confidently at our enemies and tell us what to do.

"Yah, yah," Thief suddenly hissed.

Sure enough, there was movement. It was hard to see at first, but someone or something was coming from the woods, from the direction of the village. In a moment we could make out a Stray running up to the leader.

"Message," Feelah muttered.

After a few heartbeats the leader faced the ship. He shook his fist at us. Thief jumped up to answer back, but I hauled him down.

"Watch," Feelah growled.

The leader crouched to the sand, his movement copied immediately by the rest of the Strays. In a swirl of white they began a hasty retreat back toward the safety of the trees. The ash-covered bodies seemed to blur the closer they got to the woods, as if the crest of a wave had made its way to the forest. The wave broke where the trunks were thickest, and the Strays disappeared as quickly as they had come.

"Where are they going?" Pippa strained to look more closely into the woods. "Something is making them fear. It is why they have not followed us."

I grunted. "What could they be afraid of? The Outside soldiers left many days ago, and the Spears are all dead."

The woods seemed to grow darker.

Thief growled.

I shrugged. "What can it be?" Everything appeared calm. The mountain looked as always, even though I was not used to seeing it in the dark. Nothing moved along the coastline to our left. Other than the retreating Strays, I could see nothing unusual.

"There is something near," Pippa answered. "Something that could frighten the Strays badly."

"There is no sense to it," I said. "Why would they leave us alone? They have attacked us for the last three nights. And now, when we are without the protection of fire or trees, they run away to hide in the woods."

She nodded. "There is no sense to it . . . that we can see." She looked back over her shoulder, where Tia sat, weeping bitterly. A few Onesies had gathered around her, touching her hair and wiping her tears with their small hands. There were others to comfort as well. Bran was not the only one not to make it to the ship.

We fell silent. Other than the footprints left in the moonlight there was no sign the Strays had even been there. Already the tide was out and the beach looked so much closer than it had before.

I had never been on the ship at night. Only during the

day had we started the slow work of preparing it for the voyage. At first Tia was concerned that the Strays might think we were planning something as they watched silently from the woods. In her wisdom she taught us to always have Diggers leaping and diving over the sides, making as much noise as possible. The Strays never knew that while some of us played, others were at work.

"Do we go?" Feelah asked, interrupting my thoughts. She pointed to open ocean.

I nodded, wishing again that Tia was saying the words. "When the light comes. The rocks hide beneath the waves, and we will need the sun to find our way safely." Then I turned to Pippa. "Thief and I will go to look for Bran when we have our strength back. We will search the water. If he is dead, we will tow him here so his sister can see him. She may even want to come with us if it is her wish. She is in confusion now, I fear." I sighed. "It may also be that Bran is just hurt and hiding in the grass somewhere. But if he is with the Strays, there is nothing we can do."

Pippa gazed at the moon. "We must not fall asleep. Even if the Strays are gone for now, I have no faith that they will stay away." She squeezed her eyes tight. "And there is a shadow over my heart that is not only grief. Something else is out there."

I blinked longer than I should have at the word "asleep." For a long while I stared at the beach, but the far trees remained quiet and the water lapped soothingly against the ship. The night had grown still, even in the short time we had been sitting.

Tia sniffled in the darkness.

"Curse Bran," I suddenly whispered.

Pippa's head lifted.

"Curse him! We made it to the ship, we are finally ready to sail away, and he is not here."

"He wanted to be."

"I have waited long for this." I pointed to the deck. "To be away from Strays and Spears and shards. Now Bran has ruined it. He was supposed to be here."

I felt her finger on my lips. "Then he truly was your friend. You are not used to that yet—you have had only me. It has not been easy for you since the day Bran and Tia arrived, and I fear there are many things we will have to learn about the Outside ways."

Tia and a group of Diggers lay in a huddle, their grief

already chasing them to their dreams. Eventually Pippa leaned more heavily against me, her breathing slow and gentle. It had been one of the longest days of my life, and the sorrows of the night had not made it any less tiring. I did not have the heart to wake her.

My own eyelids drooped. "No sleep . . . ," I mumbled.

3

A PAIN WAS IN MY CHEST. I TRIED to shift to move Pippa away, but the pain suddenly slipped under my throat. For a brief moment I thought we were still in the woods and that a stick was digging into me. I opened my eyes. Sleep fell away like a cast-off work-cloth.

The frowning mask of a Spear blotted out the light. Its eyeholes stared back as cold as morning water and I felt the scrape of a blade under my chin. Powerful hands held the weapon fast, the arms lost in the blackness of the long cape that hung down below his knees, over his boots. When I swallowed, the weight of the blade pushed against my throat, stretching my skin to breaking. I could not move and my breath had long since stopped.

Fear, frustration, and confusion raged through me. We had come so close. Why was there a Spear leaning over me? We had seen their bodies lying on the mountain days ago.

The blade's tip began moving again, following the line of my jaw to the opposite side of my head. The frowning mask seemed to stare a little more deeply, tilting to one side. A seabird flew high above us and when my eyes flickered to follow, the blade pushed cruelly.

"Pippa." I nudged her awake. My voice escaped like a breath of wind through a hole in a rock.

She stirred.

The helmet turned swiftly to my cellmate without the blade moving so much as a finger. I could feel Pippa's head twist, her face lifting to see our attacker. Her fingers dug into me through my work-cloth.

"Do not move," I whispered again.

All she managed was a tiny squeak. Her fingers froze.

The blade moved against my jaw, lifting this time. Then the Spear did it again with enough urgency for me to understand. Slowly I sat up, Pippa rising with me, never taking my eyes off the mask. The blade led us to our feet. Pippa clung to me tightly, our bodies moving so closely it was difficult to tell who was shaking more.

I could now see that ropes had been flung over the side railing. The tip of a rowboat was barely visible beyond the Spear's caped shoulder. The tide was out and the beach began only fifty strides from our ship. Footprints filled the sand leading to the woods and I counted at least five Spears waiting at the water's edge, sunlight glinting off their weapons.

It was clear now why the Strays had left the beach. The scent or sound of the approaching Spears must have given the messenger enough time to report their coming, so the Strays could melt back into the forest without being seen. Once the Spears reached the beach they would have seen the results of our struggle with the Strays. Everything pointed to the ship, especially the floating bundles cast free in our rush to escape.

There was a long silence. Then footsteps approached from behind. My skin tingled and fear rose in my throat, but I had been a captive long enough to know not to turn around. The Spear in front of us released one hand from his weapon and his blade moved down to my chest again. He reached out toward Pippa.

My heart lurched. A second blade slipped under my chin from behind. Like the first, it was made of shard, sharpened cruelly and with much skill. I knew the Spears' blades well—they could cut through leather as easily as brushing a hand through the air. Thief had found such a knife in the burned-out village. I swallowed heavily and shifted my weight, ready to spring.

"Wait, Corki," Pippa pleaded. "They have never hurt us when we don't move."

I stopped, letting the blade hold me in place.

The gloved hand moved closer. The Spear gripped Pippa roughly around the neck and spun her so that her back was to him. Expecting him to search for weapons, I was surprised when he took hold of her braid. He looped a finger through one of the plaits and tugged once or twice, as if testing the quality.

My eyebrows rose.

Then the fingers left Pippa and swung over to grip my work-cloth. The strength in the Spear's arm forced me to take a step backward to hold my balance. He rubbed the material near my neck several times, pulling the hood at the back over my head. Then he flipped it off again.

Standing so close, I was surprised even more by his lack of height. In the fields of Grassland where we had worked each day, the Spears were tall, at least five or six hand-spans greater than any of us. But this frowning mask stood only three hand-spans taller—closer to Tia's height than a Spear's.

"What is he doing?" I managed to ask Pippa.

"I do not know," she whispered.

And then something else caught my eye. At the center of his chest where the folds of his black cape parted, a painted red symbol stood out against his armor. A closed fist. I glanced at Pippa.

She saw it too. "They have not been Spears long," she whispered.

"How many are there?"

"Twelve. Three at least are Red Fist. Can't see the others. They are facing away from me."

Before I could think more on it, the Spear stepped back suddenly and slapped his chest. The movement frightened both of us so badly that Pippa threw her hands in front of her face and I waited for the blade to plunge into me. The Spear remained frozen in salute. The second blade left my throat.

"They are bringing everyone over to the side," Pippa said, peeking out from her fingers. Her head turned slightly away from me.

"Why?" I risked a whisper.

She twisted as far as she dared. Her voice shook when she finally answered. "They are being careful with us, taking no chances. I do not know what they mean to do with us."

"They will do whatever they want, Pippa—they are Spears," I sputtered. There was more movement beside me and I longed to turn my head to find out what the Spears were doing. Yet even without my eyes I could guess what was about to happen. Tears began to swell but I swallowed them back in anger. "They are taking us back to Grassland."

The Spear at attention suddenly spun his weapon down, pressing it against my ribs. It stung terribly and I dared not speak another word. I stared hard at the frowning mask.

"Our turn," Pippa said.

We were pushed up against the railing to join the others. There must have been forty or so who had made it to the ship, and with all the Spears added to our number, the ship listed heavily in the water. Three or four Diggers down from me I could see Thief from the corner of my eye. His thin face was drawn even tighter than usual and his hands were clenched at his sides. His knife was nowhere to be seen and I wondered if he had managed to hide it before being taken. Feelah was pressed against him, her wide nose flaring. I found myself searching for Bran before I remembered the evil of the previous night.

Without a guard in front to stop me, I strained to see behind us. They were definitely new Spears, all of them. One of the Red Fists, on my left, brought forward a leather bag the size of a seal. As he turned it over, thin straps the length of my arm spilled onto the deck like writhing sea snakes. Our guards bent one by one to pick up a handful of the leather bindings.

"For what purpose?" I muttered to Pippa.

A frowning Spear walked up to the nearest Digger. Crossing the boy's wrists in front of him, he took a rough leather strap and began to bind them. The rest of us watched in silence as the leather swished into knots. Then the Spear moved on to the next Digger. When it was our turn the strap bit into my skin and I chewed my cheek not to cry out.

Pippa will be very upset, I thought. She did not like having her hands tied. I glanced around again. We were all together, pushed up in two or three lines against the railing nearest the beach. Despair hung in most of the faces, although here and there I could see little fires of fury burning in some Diggers' eyes. Tia stood out tall and I tried to catch her attention. From the ugly red mark across her cheek I guessed that she at least had not woken peaceably. She took her place about seven or eight Diggers away.

I glanced over the rail to the swirling water below. The tide was completely out now and the ship rode the gentle swells easily. It would not be difficult to load us into small boats and take us back to land. There were ropes to cling to, and even with tied hands I imagined how I could use my feet against the sides of the ship to help guide us down. Pippa could hold on to me, if they let us.

The Digger next to me gave my shoulder a nudge. I looked at his eyes, then down to his hands. *Danger.*

I shook my head. *Boats*, I signed, nodding toward the land.

Danger, he signed again. He stared behind us.

I turned. Instead of preparing us to go into the rowboats as I expected, the Red Fists began to form their own line behind us at mid-deck. Their heavy boots stepped in rhythm until they stood shoulder to shoulder, strength for strength.

"Pippa, can you see this?" I called.

Her voice trembled. "Yes."

"Coriko!" It was Tia. Her voice was husky and worn. It was the first time she had spoken since Bran had disappeared.

"I am here."

"Can you see what they are doing? I cannot move my shoulders at all."

I twisted farther. "They are walking slowly toward us. Their weapons are pointed at our backs. All of them are behind us except for the two nearest you. Everyone is pushing. Can you ask Feelah to tell everyone to stop?" I shoved a Digger with my shoulder when he stumbled too close for my liking. The chests of those behind us pushed into our backs and the lines grew tighter. My stomach pressed against the railing.

"The Spears are coming closer, Tia. Stay with me, Pippa!" I warned.

"I am trying!" Pippa called back. Already another Digger had squeezed between us. Soon we were packed in so close, every twitch was held in check by the shoulders of someone else. Only the railing stopped me from going over the side. Fearful murmurs began to grow while we waited, heads craned to see what the Spears were doing.

"Now I am afraid," Pippa whimpered. Even though she was no longer leaning against me I could see her shoulders trembling. "Now I am very afraid."

"Stay strong, stay strong," I muttered. A tremor shook my legs.

Above us, the gulls cried their morning song, dipping and swinging easily around the ship, as carefree as they had been the night before. I could taste their freedom and cursed myself again for falling asleep.

With no warning the two Spears standing at attention by the railing suddenly tossed their weapons to waiting hands behind us. Cleaving a wedge between the side of the ship and the crowding Diggers, they forged a path with their powerful arms. Diggers fell back, held to their feet only by those behind them. To my horror the frowning Spears reached for the nearest Digger.

Grabbing arms, hair, clothing they lifted him off his feet. He kicked wildly, trying to stay on the deck. Before I could call out a warning the Red Fists turned the boy in the air so that his head faced the sea, and they flung him over the side. His wailing cry ended with a splash.

"No! Please, no!" Pippa wept. Her voice trailed off and she stared terrified at the straps around her wrists.

I could feel my teeth beginning to chatter, the blood pounding in my head. The others panicked too, jostling and pushing to get away from the railing. But there was nowhere to go. Each step backward only brought us closer to sharp blades and waiting Spears.

I spread my feet farther apart to keep control of the pushing around us. Someone fell beside me. Our whole row leaned hard to the left and I was pulled with the rest on top of the fallen Digger. It was impossible not to step on him. There was no other place for my feet to go. Even above the noise of panic a sickening crack told me a bone had broken.

"Corki!"

Pippa was down. I could see her yellow hair in between the feet of others as they swarmed over her. What was left of the line behind us broke in a frenzy and Diggers pressed dangerously all around her.

I threw an elbow at the nearest one and caught him in the throat. It earned enough space to send a kick at one more. The deck was treacherous with morning dew and my feet slid awkwardly with each step. Three people had tripped over Pippa.

"Put your hands above your head!" I yelled to her. "Hunch down, like a rock!"

She obeyed. Someone's arm struck me and blood rushed to my nose.

More hands were grasping at me as all of us struggled to keep our balance. Those at the back pushed us forward while the rest of us tried to keep away from the railing.

"I am coming, Pippa!" I flung someone else over my knee before I finally stood above her. Planting my feet on either side of her I pushed other Diggers out of the way.

"Get up, Pippa. Hurry."

She got to her feet, using me as a ladder. Her beautiful

woman's robe was torn in several places and her braids had come loose.

"Quickly, now!"

A dark shadow spread across my face.

"Beware, Corki!"

Yet even as she spoke strong hands gripped my hair. I gasped in pain. Pippa was being pulled away.

"No!" I yelled and threw an elbow behind me. My neck was jerked back farther so that I could see only the top of Pippa's head. I watched a second Spear hoist her over his shoulder and start for the railing. She kicked and squirmed with little success against his grasp.

"Corki! Corki!" Her voice rose in terror as the Spear knocked her hands aside and lifted my Pippa into the air. Reaching back and twisting, I bit into the gloved hand holding my head. There was a painful grunt.

When I turned, Pippa's golden hair flashed again in the sun, high above the others. She called my name one more time, then disappeared from sight into the waiting sea.

4

ILTHY SPEARS! FILTHY STRAYS! Curse you all!" I tried to wriggle free. Just as quickly the Spear cuffed my ear so hard, the screaming around me was drowned by a ringing that seemed to sing straight out through my hair.

When my head cleared, I tried to bite again. The Spear would not let go of my hair. He was trying to turn me around so that he could drag me backward. I kicked halfheartedly at his knee, only to be hit again. But I did not care what he did to me. I needed to get to Pippa before she drowned.

At the foot of the railing we stopped. Diggers were now leaping into the water, no longer waiting for the Spears. The Red Fists pressed closer. Their helmets flashed above the Diggers' heads, and in between their arms and legs I could see booted feet, stepping firmly, unstoppable.

To my surprise, my captor let me scramble up. The moment I gained my balance his hands left my head to clamp around my waist. With a powerful heave he sent me tumbling through the air and toward the ocean.

My back struck the water and I went under, twisting to find the bottom. It was far too deep to stand. I raised my hands above my head and kicked hard with my legs but it was difficult to get a rhythm without the power of my arms. I forced myself to relax, allowing my body to float upward.

When my head finally broke the surface I gulped in deep breaths, gasping to suck in the sky. Droplets blurred my vision and one of my braids came loose, covering one eye.

"Pippa!" I yelled the moment I had breath. I shook my head to clear the hair out of my way. Diggers splashed around me, some madly as they struggled to keep afloat. One dark head floated facedown in the water—a boy. The matted hair made me think of Bran. A moment later another body, only a few arm lengths away, came floating toward me. A girl.

"Pippa, where are you?" I screamed. The floating Digger was almost past. Despite my haste to find Pippa, I knew she would never forgive me if I did not do something. Flipping over onto my back, I made my way over to the drowning girl. She was difficult to turn over. In the end I treaded water at her side, gripped one end of her work-cloth, and slowly pulled her body over. When the air hit her face she coughed and retched up water. Her legs began treading immediately and I helped keep her head afloat with my shoulder.

"Pippa!" I tried again.

"Coreeko!" Thief's voice rang out somewhere closer to the ship.

"Thief! I am here."

"Coreeko!"

The girl beside me began to turn over.

"Stay on your back, you little idiot! Do you want to drown?"

She stared at me, her eyes wider than shells. She did not seem to know I was there.

I raised myself as high as I could to look for Pippa. At the shore more Spears stood waiting for the first Diggers to flop exhausted onto the sand. They knew their work well. None of us would have the strength to fight or run by the time we made it to the beach. Again I searched the water for my cellmate.

Moments later, to my great relief, Pippa and Thief floated over to me, both of them face up to the sky.

"Pippa, all is well?"

She was concentrating hard on her breathing. "All is well. But I want to get to shore. I do not like these." She lifted her hands. "I cannot think without my hands."

I nodded. "We must go to shore with the others," I said. "There is nowhere else for us. We will think of something when we get there."

"Coreeko," Thief gasped. "Feelah—"

"Where is she?"

"We could not find her," Pippa said. "But she will be all right. She is a good swimmer, even better than you. How much farther?"

"Thirty strides or so." I nodded at the girl floating beside me. "And I will need help with her."

We placed the girl between Thief and me, and with Pippa's encouragement managed to keep her on her back and kicking. Several times she went under and we were forced to stop and set her right.

"Is she *trying* to drown?" I sputtered.

"She is afraid, Corki," Pippa said. "And she is tired."

"So am I."

"Only a little farther."

It was agony to swim without hands, and by the sounds of the others gasping I could tell they were struggling as hard as we were. What felt like far more than thirty strides later, my feet found sand. The Spears had closed their line on the beach to a half circle. They watched us as we staggered onto firmer ground.

Ahead of us, Diggers were lying or sitting silently like bundles washed ashore. But what froze my blood and stopped me from taking one step more was the sight of their upper bodies. They were missing their heads.

"P-P-Pippa."

She squinted. "Peace, Corki. It is not what it seems. They are alive."

Still, I did not move.

"They have put coverings over their faces so that they cannot see," she said.

"Maybe we should stay in the water."

Thief was eyeing the prisoners. He grunted, then nodded toward a figure on the shore. "Feelah."

Sure enough, his cellmate was seated in the group of Diggers nearest us. There was no sign of Tia.

"We cannot leave them," Pippa said.

I groaned, still trying to get my breath. The woods were close, possibly near enough to run to. How many Spears would follow if we tried to get away? But there was no time even to talk about it, for Thief splashed ahead in an effort to reach Feelah.

"We are walking right back to them." I slapped the water with my fists. Pippa sloshed through the shallows, her gown clinging to her body like layers of seaweed. She fell to the sand. I knelt beside her, only an arm's length from the pointed end of the nearest weapon.

Our eyes met and she read my heart. "Be patient, Corki," she gasped. "Don't make them angry. Not now. Do this for me."

"I want us to be away from here," I growled.

"I know. It will happen. Just not yet."

The sharp face of the mountain seemed to mock us as more Diggers splashed ashore. But I would not leave Pippa. When a Spear thrust a sack over my head I let my shoulders slump, relieved that for the moment I could not see the peaks of Grassland laughing at us.

5

THEY MOVED US INTO THE woods. The light and heat left us as we entered the trees, and prickly fingers of dried leaves crunched with every step of our feet. Under the leaves, the earth was hard, packed smooth like the floors of our tunnels in the mountain. My hands were still tied, and when I reached out to find Pippa, I discovered that the Red Fists had linked us by yet another leather strap, just long enough to enable us to walk separately.

It was frustrating not being able see where we were going. I twisted my head, hoping to find a hole somewhere within the sack's tight weave. Nothing. I flung my head back, trying to peer out from the bottom of the sack. The motion threw me off balance and backward. Pippa gasped as the strap joining us grew taut with my weight.

"What are you doing?" she whispered.

"Sorry." I found my feet again.

We marched on. The sound of our steady shuffle and the creak of leather boots beside us formed images in my head. I wondered how those in front knew where we were going, and then I imagined a Spear at the lead, likely holding the front end of the strap in his hand. I stared at my hands. They had never tied us like this in Grassland, even when they took us into the Mouth when we entered the caves at the end of a day of digging for shards. There was nowhere to escape to, nowhere to go.

Sweat trickled onto my lips and I licked at it greedily, desperate for anything to soothe the scrape in my throat. I would have drunk ocean water if they had offered it to us. My arms and legs felt heavy and my stomach roared hungrily.

Walking behind Spears was painfully familiar and I found myself listening for the sounds of Grassland— the echoes of our tunnels or the tinkle of shards being dumped into piles. But the birds overhead sang songs of wood, leaf, and stream, not the music of the sea that I was used to.

It did not take long for me to realize that we were headed away from the shard-filled grasses to the north of the mountain. At first the wind came from behind us, blowing off the ocean and gusting against our backs. Then, as we walked through twisting forest paths, the breeze gradually began to blow against my left side. After a while it changed again and blew on our right. Then the Red Fists turned us yet again, up a small hill, and the wind fell against our backs, only to change moments later back to our left.

They mean to tire us out, I thought. *We are walking in a circle.*

As we marched my thoughts raced, sometimes forward and sometimes back, always in a jumble of worry and anger. I did not like the Red Fists. It worried me that there were no regular Spears among this group. The Red Fists were too swift in their decision-making, and from their actions on the boat it was clear they made no distinction between Onesies, Twosies, and Threesies.

Someone sobbed behind me. The sound made me think of Bran, and for a brief moment I wondered if he had eventually made it to the ship, or back to the stream-trees to hide. I strained to listen. Amid the dry coughs and gasps I recognized another sound growing louder. A stream.

"Water," Pippa whispered.

The air suddenly felt cooler against my bare shoulders. The line slowed. There was an outburst from the Diggers ahead and I tensed, ready to fight. A rough hand gripped my head from behind and the sack was ripped off. I blinked at the patterned light shining onto the forest floor. Pippa's hair was matted to her head and her face was flushed. When I tried to move closer the straps on either end went taut and held us apart. Guards were spaced evenly down our line, with a large group of them taking up the rear. A glance back showed one of them continuing down the line, yanking the sacks off the remaining Diggers.

The stream gurgled beside us. I was so thirsty I bent toward it, and when the Red Fists made no move to stop me, I fell to my knees. The straps strained, pulling one arm, then the other, as the rest of the Diggers sank to the ground beside the water. Pippa leaned forward, maneuvering the straps between us skillfully so that we managed to reach the flowing stream.

I plunged my head into the water and drank deeply. Droplets blurred my sight when I sat up.

"All is well?" Pippa made an attempt to smile. Her robe was still wet from the ocean. I wondered how she had managed to walk at all.

Our fingertips touched. The Digger behind me was still drinking and the pull on his strap made him lose his balance and splutter. I waited as a Red Fist walked past, making his way to the front of the column. "I am hungry," I said quietly. "I would eat that sack if I had it back again."

She nodded.

"And I was wrong. We are walking away from Grassland. At first they walked us in circles to get us tired, but now I have no thinking about where they are taking us. It is somewhere to the east."

She followed my eyes forward, staring at the black cape of a Red Fist. "They are like shallow water, these young Spears."

I raised my eyebrows.

"They are shiny and clear as they move about, but the inside has no depth."

"What do you mean?"

Her next words came more quietly. "They are not like the old Spears. These ones are strong in a *weak* way. Like a young whale coming too close to the shore. It does not know what it is doing, but it is confident because it is young."

I nodded. "I feel that too."

"It makes them dangerous, I think."

I looked at my cellmate. "Can you walk in those woman clothes? You look as if you will fall with every step."

She sniffed. "It will dry."

"Lean closer and I will rip off the bottom. Then at least you can walk without falling."

"You will not!"

"What will you do if you fall? The Red Fists will rip the whole thing off you."

She touched the cloth. "If we are to die now, then I want to die in this." She smoothed the soaking cloth.

"Not in a Digger's work-cloth, and not in a torn woman's robe."

I checked for Red Fists, then turned back to her. "It is already torn. There and there." I pointed. She lifted the folds to peer at the holes. "Lean toward me," I said.

"Maybe you can fix them . . ."

I shook my head. "I do not have the skill. Lean toward me."

She touched the cloth again, then reluctantly slid her legs in my direction. I tugged the leather strap hard to gain some slack on the Digger behind me, then reached out and took hold of the cloth at Pippa's mid-thigh. She jerked her hands down and whacked at me. "That is too high! There will be nothing left."

"You have to be able to run," I whispered. I took hold of the cloth around her knees. It tore easily enough as I wrapped it around my fist. Twice I had to stop as a Spear passed.

"What a waste of cloth," I muttered. "This is too hot to wear in the sun."

"You liked it well enough when I wore it in the moonlight. Have you forgotten?"

56

It was true. The first time I had seen her in the woman robe was outside the ruined Spear village after we had first escaped. It had stunned me to see Pippa look so different. She had not worn it again until yesterday.

When I did not answer she said more quietly, "You have probably forgotten." She looked away.

I sighed. "I have not forgotten. But look at us, Pippa." I tugged on the strap to make her turn. "Look at all of us." I held up my tied hands. "How can you think of robes and kisses when the Red Fists are here?"

"*That* is why we *should* think of them," she answered. "Think of Bran. Remember what happened, so suddenly, so quickly? We do not know how long we have." Her eyes went to my mouth. "Always remember robes and kisses, Corki. Remember all the things we had, even if only for a short time. No matter what happens, remember."

Her hands jerked without a warning, pulling us off balance. The Diggers were standing. Red Fists marched down the length of our line on either side, their long weapons flashing in and out of sunlight. We began a slow shuffle, finding a pace where the straps were spaced evenly enough to allow us to move faster. I waited for

57

the sacks to be put back over our heads, but nothing happened. It felt gloriously cool to have the air on my face and fresh water still trickling into my mouth from my wet hair.

I smiled to see Pippa's legs bare now in front of me. She would not be pleased with the ragged edges, but at least she would not trip over the cloth. Then I looked back down the line, searching in vain for Tia or Thief.

"Where are the others?" I whispered. Pippa shook her head. We walked in silence again and I noticed that the shadows of the forest had grown longer. They had kept us going in circles long into the afternoon, but now they moved us with a purpose. There was a different smell to these woods, an older scent that made me think of ancient trees and buried stone. The trunks were huge, gnarled, and knotted. I could not smell the sea.

Many, many paces later the line stopped. I stood on my toes and looked over Pippa's head past the slouching backs of the others. The woods thickened to form a wall of brush on either side of us, so deep I could not see through it. The Spears let us sit again and we waited out the day, resting our backs uneasily against the impenetrable walls of hedge. Whatever it was we were waiting for was only a hundred strides farther, for up ahead I could see the sun streaming into a clearing surrounded by towering trees.

"Get up, Pippa," I whispered. We stepped forward, falling once again into the plodding pace the strap allowed. It was a short march. The wall of brush ended suddenly and our faces were bathed in waning sunlight. Pippa shuddered. We stood in a large open circle with thinning grass under our feet and a smoldering fire pit at the circle's center. It was a dreary place. The ground ahead was gray with ash, as if no living thing could make its way up through the soil to color the earth. A troop of ancient trees, so tall I could hardly see their tops, stood like sentinels at the circle's edge.

Pippa began to shake and I followed her gaze to the nearest of the old trunks. Blackened by fire and cut by rope marks, it looked as much a captive of the grove as we were to the Spears. Wear marks had smoothed the bark, and here and there where fire had not reached it, the bark was stained dark red. "Ashes and fire," she said. "This is an evil place."

I turned to the next great trunk and found the same markings as on the first. Pain and suffering seemed to seep from the twisting wood, and the leaves high overhead rustled ominously. Our line had come to a quaking halt, and frightened heads turned to all sides, glancing from one tree to the next. Carrion crows filled the branches, peering down from their height, flapping and stamping expectantly.

Pippa stooped and reached to touch the ground. "It is here."

I knelt as well to see what she was looking at.

In her palm she sifted a handful of ash. The gray flakes stood out pale against her dirt-stained fingers. "This is where it happens."

My body tensed and I found myself wanting to be closer to the fire pit, away from the looming trees. I stood again, clenching my fists.

She held my eyes for a moment, then looked up over my shoulder to the sky above. "My dreams have caught up with us," she whispered. "This is the Separation." The ash in her palm caught and swirled in a sudden gust of breeze, spilling out onto the colors of her dress.

Her gaze moved to the fire pit. "It would be wise for me to pray now, I think."

The Red Fists charged before her words could become a prayer.

6

THE STRAPS KEPT US FROM escaping. As each of us turned to run in a different direction, the wild pulling flung most of us onto our faces. My cheek slammed to the earth while my arms were twisted underneath me. For a brief moment Pippa was lying beside me, her eyes huge and staring, until she was jerked away like a caught fish on a stick.

A knee pressed into my back, and the edge of a black cape suddenly swept across my sight. I felt a blade against my wrist, worrying at the leather straps until my hands came free. I was pulled to my feet with one of my arms twisted behind my back. It wasn't until I was pushed toward the trees that the guards came even with me, their broad shoulders pressing in on either side. Everywhere I looked, black capes swirled and Diggers writhed or stumbled to the edge of the grove, all the older males being led to the ancient trees. With the last of my strength I dug my heels into the ground to keep away from their menacing branches.

Voices screamed behind me, girl voices and Onesie voices. I was thrown against the rough bark. Burned wood crumbled against my face, filling my nose with the smell of fire and smoke. Then the Spears turned me, pressing my back against the trunk. Ropes were fastened to my hands. Two frowning Spears moved swiftly in front of me, binding cords across my chest and pinning me ever more tightly against the tree. I could not move my arms or legs. Specks of bark clouded my eyes and I felt tears forming.

The girls were huddled near the fire pit at the center of the grove. Five or six guards faced them, and despite my blurry vision I found Pippa's yellow hair amid the black and brown. The Onesies cried out in terror as Spears led them out the same way we had entered. *They were taking the Onesies.* I shook my head to clear my sight.

On either side of me Diggers were still being tied to trees. They were Twosies, all of them. The ropes binding them fastened onto pegs at the sides of each trunk. The weaves looked strong and were tied with the kind of skill that only knife or shard could work through. Thief was three trees away. His chin sagged to his chest, but at least he was alive. My heart gave a leap at the sight of him.

When the last Digger was fastened securely to his tree, the Red Fists surprised us again. Like the Strays only a short night before, they melted into the thicker woods behind us, all moving at the same speed, swift and sure-footed. The guards around the girls also backed away, walking slowly toward the trees, watching our cellmates until the blackness of their capes was swallowed by the greater shadow of the woods.

A silence filled the grove, a stunned quiet, as if each of us had been slapped by an unseen hand. So quickly had the Spears done their work that my thinking was still trying to catch up. The pain of the day weighed heavily on me, and as much as they cut into my skin, I was thankful for the ropes that held me upright. The only sound was the rustling of the leaves above and the creak of the trunks at our backs, swaying in the wind. The girls remained frozen, staring at the woods, too tired or afraid to move. Even the crows were still now, hunkered tightly like a hundred black apples filling the branches.

The sun had sunk even lower, but a shaft of light pierced the forest and fell on the face of the Digger pinned nearest the opening into the grove. His braids had somehow remained tied despite the wildness of our day, and I wondered if it was Pippa's work that held them. The sun caught the ocean salt stained white on his dark skin, giving him the bonelike appearance of a Stray. More heads turned toward him, and together we watched the light move over his face, so slowly, until the last of the sunlight was gone. As if on signal the black watchers fled their perches in a rush of wings and raucous clacking.

It was terrible to watch the sun leave us. When the boy's face fell into shadow a chill spread over my heart. Darkness would follow quickly.

Pippa stood among the girls. I could see her determined step breaking the circle of the others. She made her way straight for me. She glanced about, eyeing the nearest trees without changing her pace. When she was only ten strides away from me, the remaining girls rose too, each one setting out in the direction of her mate. A tiny cluster stayed seated, no more than five. For the first time since the ship we could see clearly who had lost cellmates.

Pippa kept coming. Her small hand stroked my face the moment she reached me. Tears flowed before I could stop them and I squeezed my eyes shut. My shoulders would not stop shaking.

"Peace. Peace, Corki." I felt a soft edge of her dress rubbing the dirt off my cheek. "You have soot on your nose, too."

I found my voice, but it trembled like a Onesie's. "How can this be a place of peace?"

She wiped the tears away as well, then ran her fingers through my hair as if we were lying in our cell in Grassland. "Where two stand in peace together," she whispered, "it is a place of peace. No matter what is around them. And here we are"—she looked over her shoulder—"many more than two."

"They have taken the Onesies, Pippa."

"I know."

"Your dreams were right—ashes and dust. Did you know what this . . . ?"

She sighed. "Yes, I knew it before we even came to this

place." She did not need to say the words. We both knew them. *The Separation.*

How the horror of those words weighed on my heart after years of hoping that the time would not come. "They will take me away from you."

She nodded, confirming what all of us knew too well. When Diggers reached the age of a Threesie, thirteen or so summers, they were Separated from their cellmates. We never saw any of them again. I had watched enough Threesies be taken from the cells to have the vision forever locked in my fears.

I pushed my cheek against Pippa's hand and closed my eyes, pretending that we were far from the evil grove, far from Spears and far from danger.

"I do not think I can undo the ropes," Pippa said. She followed the cords to the side of the trunk.

"No, they are well tied."

"Should I look for some food? There was fruit in the stream-trees before. Perhaps there is some here as well."

I shook my head. "The Red Fists cannot be far—they must be close by in the trees. They would not risk leaving us alone. You should not go in there by yourself."

"I could take some girls with me."

"It is not good thinking. Did you see Feelah? Is she with the others?"

"Yes. And Tia, too. Her strength is returning but I fear for her. Her anger is so deep that she will not wait long to do something." She sighed and leaned her head against my chest. "Does it hurt when I do this?"

"No."

We listened to each other breathing for a while, waiting. I could hear whispers across the grove as cellmates spoke in fearful tones at the gathering dark. The moon peeked just above the trees surrounding the grove, clothed in wisps of black cloud that lifted briefly from time to time to bare its face. I strained at the ropes, but there was not even a hint of slack.

Pippa stirred and mumbled.

"Pippa?"

"Hmmm?"

"Are you sleeping?"

"No."

"What are you doing?"

"Praying."

I heaved again at the cords. "Why? Why are you praying?"

Silence.

"I am still tied to a tree, Pippa. I can do nothing to stop them when they come back. They are dangerous, these young Spears. You know that. They will do with us what they will. How has praying helped? Nothing has been good, everything is bad, and we are going to die in these trees."

She did not say anything for a moment. Her hand reached behind me and I could hear her fingers brushing the bark. Then she sighed. "I love you."

I would not look at her.

She pulled my chin so that I had to turn. "I said, I love you. I love you, I love you, I love you."

My anger began to shift, seeping from the front of my head, then out through my back into the tree. My face felt flushed. "Shhh. Be quiet, Pippa. Why are you saying this?"

She stood on her toes to look into my eyes. "I love you," she whispered so quietly it tingled my ears. She kissed my lips.

In that horrible place, with death lurking so near, her words spoke clear.

"Yes," I answered. I kissed her back as best I could.

She nodded, her eyes unclouded and bright. "I do not know if happy or sad things will follow this night. But I know that when I pray my love gets stronger, even before the words are out of my mouth. The hate goes away. And there is a comfort. A comfort that someone bigger than the Spears is watching us with kind eyes."

I looked over her head, where the first stars of the night were beginning to wake. Here and there groans erupted from the grove, and the sound of weeping rose to the trees.

"I hope that is true, Pippa."

She leaned against me again and began to speak softly, the way she used to tell stories as we lay on the straw in our cell. Although it was familiar I did not think that I had heard this tale before.

"A long time ago when there was nothing, not even the sea or the sky, the Maker breathed air into the world. Water sprang up to become seas, and the lands were made into mountains and plains. Fish swam in the oceans and beasts roamed the newness of the grasses. People were made from the dust of the ground, male and female to stand beside one another. Breath was given to them and they grew, playing and singing with the joy of life. They could hear the voice of life in their dreams."

I focused on her voice, trying to lose the pain of the ropes in her words.

"A darkness came into the world, and shadows filled the songs of the people for the first time. Evil things were done, and the Maker's heart was grieved. The voice of life left the dreams of the people, and they and the Maker were separated. In time only those who remembered, who looked, could hear that voice in their dreams. Even now, it is said the Maker is not far from each of us." She stopped speaking and her head bobbed.

"Pippa?"

"It is something my father would say to us at night."

"I have never heard you tell that story."

I felt her sigh against my chest. "I have told you many times, but you are always asleep by the time I get to it."

"Where is the Maker now?" I asked.

"Not far."

I tried to find the moon again. The clouds we had seen earlier had thickened and were moving faster than before. "Storm must still be coming."

She turned her head away and sniffed the air. "Yes. Rain."

Storms were not frequent in Grassland, although the rains came heavily for a short time following the summer. Before long the first drops began to fall, landing with a patter on the dry leaves overhead. Above us, the stars disappeared behind vast islands of cloud. The rich scent of moist earth lifted, drowning out the acrid smell of smoke at my back. A wind picked up and the sound of quivering branches grew as loud as the rain. I could feel the trunk against my back swaying.

"Here it comes."

The water was warm, splashing off our cheeks in rivulets and bathing our faces and throats. I let the droplets gather below my tongue in order to gain a deeper drink. While it was nowhere near enough, we did not stop until our necks grew sore and our heads too heavy to lift.

"It is a gift, Corki."

"Pippa, can you wipe my eyes? I cannot shake the water away."

Her hands were mere shadows now, wiping my face. "Is that better?" She squeezed my nose.

Whether it was the kiss, the drink, or Pippa's prayer, I could not tell, but a peace came over me and I laughed. The sound must have carried, for the other Diggers hushed their talk and only my laughter mingled with the rain. Pippa laughed too and squeezed my nose again.

"Coreeko?" Thief's voice wafted back to us.

"Thief!" I yelled. I waited for a reply, trying to see through the darkness. Pippa stood down from me and faced the inner circle, turning to look for our friends. As I watched her move, the side of her face was suddenly lit by a blazing light, so bright I had to squint, and her eyebrows shot up in surprise. A dozen flaming arrows arching just below the branches of our trees flew past, heading for the center of the grove.

7

THE FIRE PIT HAD COME ALIVE. Light flickered on the face of the Digger tied to each trunk. The cluster of girls who had remained at the fire pit screamed in terror when the flames blazed up only paces away from them.

A terrible crash erupted behind us, and at first I wondered if my tree had been struck by lightning. When it came again Pippa gave a yelp and leaped back to cling to my work-cloth. Then I realized the sound was of metal. The Red Fists had returned.

"Can you see them?" I hissed.

Pippa did not say anything, so in the flickering light I searched the bushes, waiting for the black helmets and shimmering weapons to emerge. I had to clamp my jaws to keep my teeth from chattering. The clashing came again, louder and faster than before. From the fire to the woods to the fire, then back to the woods, our heads turned and turned. The rain fell steadily, shaking the branches and rattling the forest floor like a hundred feet shuffling through the brush. As the clashes grew faster, all the Diggers began to scream in terror, clinging to their cellmates.

There was a command to the beat, an urgency with each grinding note. A girl to our left fell with her face to the ground.

"Where are they?" I asked Pippa.

"I cannot see them!"

Clash! Clash! The whole grove shook with the sound, and the trees quivered with the rest of us. Still our attackers remained unseen.

Clash! Clash! Clash!

A wild thought entered my head. "What if it is not Red Fists?" I stammered.

"What do you mean?" Pippa shot a glance at me.

"What if it is not Spears? What if they left us to be killed by . . . something from the forest? Something worse?"

She turned back to look at the woods.

Still the clamor rose until, blending with the noise, I heard Diggers around me joining their voices to the hideous sound. It began as a screech from a Digger far across from us, barely heard above the crashing. Then others followed, awkwardly yelping in time with the beat. Ghastly faces seemed to hang from the trees around me, lit up by the flames, the Diggers' bodies jerking as each crash sounded. My own voice suddenly leaped out and I found myself shouting with the rest until tears streamed down my face.

Pippa alone remained still. Although I could see she was afraid, her lips moved silently in prayer. In the light of the fire I could see her hands held tightly over her ears.

I watched her mouth move but could not hear what she said, with the grove in such madness. Finally she gripped my head with both hands and yelled into my ear, "They are trying to frighten us, Corki. It is just noise. That is all. Listen to me instead."

My teeth continued to rattle but I managed to stop yelling.

"Good, Corki. Think of robes and kisses."

Robes and kisses.

She pushed her face up close to my ear and wrapped an arm around my neck. "They are coming now, Corki. Bad things will happen for a while, I think. But do not lose hope. Find me."

I could not think clearly. Her words mingled with the rain, with the storm of voices all around, with the dread that lurked behind us. I tried to listen to her, to keep from wincing every time the clashes came, but the fear was greater than my heart.

With one final horrific clash the Red Fists entered the circle of trees, bursting through the grove like hungry sharks, their armor flashing blood-red in the firelight. Figures blurred in front of us, caught in fire and shadow and smoke. Pippa was ripped from my shoulder and fell down to the crackling leaves.

I watched, unbelieving, as two Spears held her firmly between them, forcing her to stand. One of them held a wooden stake in his hands, the size of my leg. Pippa was pushed to her knees, and the Red Fist gripped her by the back of her hair. The other raised a naked sword. Dreamlike, a nightmare come alive, the weapon hung poised in the night sky.

My knees gave out completely and words stuck on my tongue. Pippa raised her eyes to me as the sword came down. The sound of its slashing was overcome by a crackle of thunder over the sea. I threw up when he lifted the sword again, knowing that my Pippa would be dead. I would not look. I did not ever want to see what was waiting for me on the forest floor. I would not believe it. Ever.

"Corki."

Robes and kisses . . . I was still hearing her voice.

"Corki. Are you all right?" I lifted my head. When my eyes came level, Pippa was exactly where she had been, staring up at me.

"They took my hair," she said.

Babble came out of my mouth. "Pippa!" I finally gasped, so happy to see her head in the right place. I followed her gaze to look at the Red Fists towering above her. One of them held a fistful of Pippa's braids in his hands, dangling it out in front of him. Then he handed the hair to the other Spear.

"All is well?" I managed to croak.

"Yes, so far. But I wish they had not taken my braids."

While we watched, one Red Fist fastened her hair to the top of the stake with a thin piece of cord, like the kind we had found in the Spear village. There was a notch in the wood that fit the cord perfectly. When he was finished he held the stake out to me, Pippa's hair almost touching my nose. Then he turned and walked back toward the fire. The guard with the sword continued to hold Pippa to the ground, but his helmet turned to follow his partner.

I glanced to my left and noticed another Red Fist doing the same thing with the girl closest to us.

A single thought managed to break through my confusion. "They will take you from me now," I whispered.

Pippa nodded, her eyes gleaming with tears. "Yes."

For many summers I had imagined this moment. Night after night in our cell, thinking what I would do, playing it out until sleep overtook me. In my dreams we had always escaped the Separation, swimming out to a friendly ship that entered the bay or crossing the desert with handfuls of dried fish to keep us alive. I had never imagined that I would be tied to a tree and my beautiful Pippa taken away right in front of me.

I looked back at her tears and anger burned up from the pit of my stomach—not welling like a growing stream but gushing like the torrents of a Cleansing. I strained at my ropes, cursing at the black helmet in front of me. When I could still not get my hands loose I twisted my head, trying in vain to get at the ropes with my teeth.

The Red Fist watched me silently, his eyes hidden by the shade of his mask. Behind him, the second guard was pounding the stake into the ground a few paces from the fire. The locks of yellow hair glinted back at me.

Pippa watched him closely, then interrupted my cursing. "Corki! Listen to me!"

My voice came out like an animal's growl. "What!"

"Look at what they are doing."

"Filthy ropes! Pippa, I cannot get loose to help you!"

"Coriko! Look at the fire pit. Can you see that he has put my hair on the stake?"

"Yes. Of course I can see it."

Her guard was standing now and raising her to her feet.

"My heart is beating quickly . . . but I think it is good he has taken my hair."

"Why?"

She glanced at her guard. "Remember White Eye?"

White Eye. I drifted back at the sound of the name, to days and days ago, when we had found the dying Red Fist in the Spear village. White Eye had been a Digger at one time. His words as a Red Fist had put a cloud over my heart ever since.

"Remember?" Pippa continued. "White Eye told us that he became a Spear at the Separation. And he said that his mate was *alive.*"

I could still remember White Eye's face as he lay dying. It was because of him that we had begun to realize the fate of all male Diggers. In time we were all made Red Fists, then eventually Spears.

The Red Fist holding Pippa took a step toward the fire. I cursed at him but he did not turn.

"Pippa!" I yelled.

She tried to peer around the Spear's arm to look at me. "I will see you again! I know it! Peace. Find me!"

The rest of her words were lost in screams as the girls were driven toward the fire pit. I saw Tia then, for the first time since the ship, standing tall on the far side of the fire pit, with no bonds on her wrists. Pippa made her way over to Tia and the two of them embraced. They raised their hands to me. A moment later Feelah joined them.

The Red Fists moved toward them slowly, their weapons lowered. Through the spaces between the Spears I could see the fearful faces watching their approach.

The fire went out suddenly in a hiss of steam and blinding smoke. The grove was plunged into darkness. The wind blew in my direction, driving the smoke into my face. I choked and gagged, still trying to see the girls. From the sounds of their voices they were moving farther away, out of the grove and into the forest. More shouting and screams followed, some of them my own, until our mates' voices grew faint.

The rain continued to fall and I shut my eyes tight, trying to listen. The other Diggers fell silent too, each of us hoping to hear beyond the dripping of the trees. But no more shouts followed. The Red Fists had left us in darkness, unprotected from the wild things of the woods. More than anything, they had taken my Pippa, and taken my heart out along with her.

PART TWO

8

THE CAPE WAS FAR TOO BIG. AND it was heavy. I let the hem sweep across the ash as I turned, then lifted it to a more comfortable height. The eye-guards of my practice helmet did not permit a full view.

"It will have to cover armor one day." Marumuk fastened the collar roughly at my neck. "And you will grow into it, as I did." He straightened and clapped the side of my helmeted head.

I stared up at him, a full five hand-spans taller than I was. In the hundred and one days I had known him, he had rarely smiled. Marumuk was a warrior. As a leader among the Spears, he did not carry the burden lightly, and I was lucky that he had chosen me.

I shifted the cape again and quickly brought my sword

arm out from under the folds, taking a swipe at an unseen enemy with my bare hand. It brought him as close to a smile as he could get.

"You are getting faster, but you would still be dead against a real warrior," Marumuk said.

"Faster than Thief," I said, watching his eyes carefully.

He glanced across the ash-covered ground of the Grove where the rest of the thralls continued to train. "You have a good master," he said quietly. His brows knotted much the way Thief's did when he was deep in thought. They were similar in other ways as well, these two. Both had the same dark skin and tight, curly hair. If it were allowed, I imagined that they could have spoken a similar language. It had surprised most of the Diggers when Marumuk had chosen a blue-eyed, white-skinned thrall.

It was difficult to find the right words. Like the rest of the Diggers, I understood more than I could speak of the Spear language. Much of what we learned at the beginning was for daily survival and warfare. Thief and I would repeat the words at night in the darkness of the

Grove, mouth to ear, while others slept. The Red Fists had little patience for error, and any advantage was worth working for. And for the first time we were able to speak to each other without our hands.

Friendship was something the masters had not expected, especially from a bedraggled group of Diggers chased out of Grassland by war. At first Thief and I had tried to hide our talking, but as the days passed we discovered that Marumuk favored us. We were allowed to fight together, and after the first ten days they let me sleep beside Thief, closer to the fire.

I bowed to Marumuk and resisted saying anything further. He was a good master. I was not beaten nearly as much as some of the other boys, nor did he ever shame me in front of the other masters. As a trainer he did not have an equal. When the Spears fought in practice it was Marumuk who always ended up with his foot on his opponent's chest. Hardly anyone could match his strength in wrestling, and no one could defeat him with a sword. It was under his teaching that I had earned the cape, the first of all the Spear equipment. But even with his favor I had come to learn that he was not safe to be around.

"If you have finished looking at yourself"—he tossed a wooden practice sword to me—"we will continue."

I caught the sword easily and raised it into guard position, feeling the strange weight of the cape around my shoulders. I faced the fire pit. All over the ash-covered ground, thralls and masters sparred with poles or wooden swords. It was easy to understand now why the earth had looked so beaten down when we first saw the Grove. At the farthest edges, where the trees grew tightly together, there were other thralls hiding in the brush. Part of each day was spent on watch, always with a master—the only time we were allowed to carry true weapons.

"Who am I fighting today?" I had learned by the end of the third day of our training that the only thing that pleased Marumuk was persistence. Persistence and success.

Light poured into the Grove from overhead as the sun reached midday. At the edge of the fire pit, Pippa's hair waved back at me from the stake. *Be well*, I prayed. *Robes and kisses.* I let my eyes linger before turning to my master.

"There will be no thrall rounds this day." He pulled his own sword and raised it, rather than the practice stick.

I eyed him warily, matching his stance and nervously keeping the wicked blade at arm's length.

"Who will I fight, then?"

He ignored my question. "What have I told you, when you are approached by a larger enemy?" He advanced slowly, powerfully, forcing me to step back with each pace.

"Find something strong to put my back against," I grunted. "Like a tree or a rock . . . or a brother."

"Why?" he growled, getting more aggressive with his blade. He slashed out and our weapons met, the metal against the wood. I watched a splinter fly from my sword. His eyes gleamed from behind his helmet.

I repeated the chant: "There is strength in stone, and two are better than one."

With a single movement he batted my weapon out of my hands and gripped the front of my cape, raising me to my toes. The Spear mask drew close to my face.

"Yes, two *are* better than one. You will understand that soon. Learn it in your heart and I will be pleased." He pushed me and I stumbled. I rolled, found my feet, then stood sharply in guard position, my weapon back in my hand. He sheathed his sword and watched me for a moment as my arms glistened with sweat.

"Come with me."

I lowered my arms slowly, my heart still pounding, ready for a fight. We moved to the center of the Grove, where several other thralls had gathered with their masters. At the sight of Marumuk the remaining fighters ceased their work and strode over to stand beside us. There was no reason for surprise at this. We often gathered at the fire pit to chant Spear words or to make the food. But this day was different—I could sense the tension in my master.

Thief looked across at me. His own cape hung heavily on his wiry frame. His black hair, unbraided, flowed from under the back of his helmet, almost to his shoulders. He looked nothing like the scrawny Digger who had come to the Grove a hundred days ago. I glanced at the hardened faces of the others around me and imagined I must look the same.

Marumuk interrupted my thinking. Like the other Spears, he kept his helmet on and his sword hand resting against the hilt.

"There has been good fighting in the last days," he

announced. He spoke the Spear language slowly, as if wanting every word to be heard well. "Four have won their capes. They have proven themselves chosen. The rest of you must do so soon." There was a hint of warning in his voice that chilled me. Thief's eyes went to the stakes around the fire pit and I followed his gaze. One had been pulled out like a gaping tooth, breaking the perfect circle. It lay flat on the soil, half covered in ash. Many days earlier one of the Diggers had fallen asleep while on watch. Although his master was only steps away, he had given in to the hard days of training and long nights of little sleep. He was beaten in front of us the next morning, and his mate's stake toppled. We never saw him again.

But it was Marumuk's next words that sent a cold finger of fear straight to my heart. I repeated them in my head to make certain I had understood correctly: "The four will be coming with us on the next march. If they succeed in their tasks, they will receive their daggers"—he eyed all the thralls—"and be allowed a time with their mates."

Pippa! I bit my lip. *A raid.*

Thief's helmet dipped.

"If they fail," he continued, "their stakes will be removed."

I eyed Thief. We knew exactly what Marumuk's words meant. There was a long silence. Then Marumuk raised his sword to the sky. "Who are you?"

All of us clapped our chests with our right fists and chanted, "We are the chosen!"

"You are the chosen," he repeated. "Fight well, die well, protect the shards."

"Fight well, die well, protect the shards!" we chanted. The words rolled off my tongue with practiced ease. Sometimes they even echoed in my head while I slept. But my thoughts were not with the words this time. Instead, they searched ahead to the coming hours and the source of dread that would not leave me day or night. Until this moment, all my efforts in training had been to keep Pippa safe, to avoid a beating, and to win the favor of my masters. Now the practices of the Grove were about to become the ways of my life. Guilt fell on me like a crow descending on a piece of wasted meat. Would we now be forced to go and steal children, even as we ourselves had been taken years ago? It was something Pippa would never do—at any cost.

But I could not, would not, lose her. *Pippa. Hide your eyes from what we will do.* I could only take comfort that she was not here to know what we were about to do.

The Red Fists said little about our mates. Only their locks of hair were the ever-present reminder of their absence. In the silence of the nights all I could think about was Pippa. I would look up past the trees of the Grove to the stars above and imagine she was beside me. I missed her small hands on the back of my neck, turning my hair into perfect braids the way none of the other girls could. I missed her face and her soothing laughter in the darkness. I had even started to pray, using the words of our Northern tongue and not the speech of Spears. Yet now the only way I would see her again was if I did the very things that would shame Pippa to her soul.

"The four will come forward," Marumuk was saying.

I stepped with Thief and the two others into the center of the Grove, only a stride from the glowing embers of the fire. I knew these thralls. In the last days of fighting I had faced each one with sword, staff, and in wrestling. The taller one was tireless, and our wrestle had lasted so long, the others were allowed to stop and watch. Neither of us could win, and Marumuk had separated us. But with swords I could beat him, and Marumuk had made me finish one of the bouts by thrusting my wooden sword so hard into his shoulder that I drew blood. He never forgot it, and often looked for ways of getting even. Thief had become my eyes and ears after that fight, for in the Grove there were many opportunities to find revenge. It did not surprise me that my opponent had earned his black cape. His name was Hammoth.

The other thrall, Rezah, was shorter than me, but stronger if I let him get in close during a wrestle. When not fighting, he was one of the few who would laugh quietly when masters were not looking. His thick woolly hair could not help but make me think of Bran. In times of mock battle, he was my first choice to fight beside whenever Thief was resting.

Holding his hand above us, Marumuk began to speak quickly, and with many words I could not understand. When he finished, the four of us were led outside the Grove toward the main path we used for running each day. Before we left, Marumuk stopped me. His eyes gleamed white behind the eye-slits of his helmet.

"I will see you before the raid," he said.

I nodded. It was rare for him to be gone long from the Grove, although it was rumored that he returned to the mountain from time to time, and despite the harshness of his training methods I had come to depend on him.

"Will you be with us on the raid?" I asked.

His eyes narrowed behind the mask. "There is only one thing for you to think about right now." As I turned to follow the others, wondering what he had meant, he called out, "Learn your ship-work well. It is the heart of the chosen."

I glanced back one last time to the fire pit, where Pippa's hair shone in the sun. "I do not like leaving her there," I whispered to Thief.

He nudged my shoulder. "She is in front of us, Coreeko. Not behind."

I did not answer him. It was forbidden to speak outside the Grove.

The moment we left the openness of the training circle, the trees thickened around us. Twisted roots, some the size of my leg, sprawled along the ground like enormous worms searching for soil. We were taken along paths we had never traveled before, and I could feel Thief's excitement growing as quickly as my own. We jogged in twos, shoulder to shoulder except for places where the woods would not allow it. In time, the wind blew in our faces and I smelled the sea. Thief reached for my arm and squeezed it as we ran. Above us, the cry of a gull broke the rustling of branches. The sea!

As we ran, questions kept rising in my thoughts. Pippa had somehow known for a long time that the Separation was coming. When it did, horrible and heartrending, it was followed morning and night with our endless fighting practices. Each day held the weight of losing a mate, the possibility of beatings, blood, and bruises. We were forced to learn the language of our masters, which confused and muddled the talk in my head. The constant training and little sleep had filled the days so quickly there was no time to think about what we were doing. I longed for just one evening to sit and think clearly. Was Pippa well? Had she angered the Spears with her stubborn kindness and fallen into harm? Had her hair grown back?

I could not protect her in whatever place they had taken her, could not comfort her, could not wipe away her tears. Tia would give her life to protect Pippa—I knew that much, and tried to comfort myself. Now my feet were carrying me toward a raid. Toward Pippa, if I did what the Spears had trained me to do. But would my Pippa ever forgive my actions, even if done to save her life?

The Spear leading us urged us to run faster. We had a task to accomplish, and more training to complete. I picked up my pace along with the others. Hard training meant staying alive, the masters often told us. If there was little mercy in the Grove, there would be even less in the world of men, where one mistake could mean a sword stuffed in your gut.

The thought of a raid terrified me. As a Digger, I had fought to protect our shards so many times that my knuckles hardly healed over before they were torn open again. Occasionally I had even used a rock against another Digger when I thought there was a danger to Pippa as we picked shards in the fields. But the fight was always against other Diggers and never with the kind of weapons we had now been trained to use. Marumuk had said little about raiding. All we knew was that it was an honor to go, and that it brought back more Diggers for picking shards.

Failure was death.

I shook my head. The ocean was closer now. I could feel moist air blowing against my skin, as it had most of my life. Our pace slowed slightly as the Red Fist in front came to a halt. *Stop,* he signed. We dropped to the ground, Thief's sweating arm sliding against my own. Directly ahead, waves pounded the beach.

Moments later we were moving again, stepping suddenly into the open and onto the hot sand. I half expected to see Pippa standing there, waving at us. Instead, two tall ships waited in a tiny harbor, listing with the surf. The beach was short, only a hundred strides. A chain of Spears passed bundles from the trees to the waiting ships. Guards were posted at either headland, and more stood on the ships' railings, their capes billowing like tiny sails.

I tried to see the mountain of Grassland, but the trees at the beachhead were so close it was impossible to look beyond them. A mist crept across the water, as it often did during this part of the year. I nodded to myself. It made good sense to go raiding when you could appear and disappear out of the clouds.

I turned my attention to the ship. It was as long as the

boat we had found at the old Spear village, with a smaller girth. There was no deck. The ship sat low in the water, and the bow rose up out of the mist in an arching neck like a sea beast, its mouth open and grinning. Places for sitting had been made along the entire length of the ship, with a center path for walking up the middle. Long pieces of wood rested against each seat, sliding out through holes in the side and into the water below. This ship was made for speed, not for carrying the burden of shards. The wood planks were gray with age and the scores and hack marks wherever my eyes fell told of battles and blood.

There was no rest. A tall Red Fist approached our group and the four of us were taken to the nearest ship. We waded into the shallow water. The cool splash against my leggings sent a shiver down my back.

The guards on board stood down from their perches and hands reached out to haul us up. It was still a strange feeling to have Spears helping me, and from the way Thief hesitated I guessed he was thinking the same. Each of us was given a bench to sit at. The guards took places behind or in front until all the seats were taken. Our capes were taken off and bundled neatly under our seats.

In one startling motion our helmets were also removed, then attached to a peg at the side of our benches. Black and brown heads shook themselves free of the weighty helms, and hair flowed around faces I did not recognize, other than those from the Grove.

I stared over the shoulder of the Spear in front of me, watching his weathered hands push down on the piece of wood at his lap as the other end rose up to become level with the side of the ship. I followed his movements, remembering Marumuk's advice to learn well. The wood was heavy, and I had to push hard to make it rise.

I could barely see above the railing. The ocean stirred restlessly and I felt the slap of waves at the back of the ship. It was nothing like the craft we had tried to escape on. This one encompassed me, my hands, my feet, and my knees pressing against one side. Hardly had I settled in my seat than the ship moved under my feet and I felt us easing clear of the beach. Twelve or more Spears stood there grunting as they shouldered the back end of the ship into the water. I glanced toward the front. I could just see the back of the sea beast's head, where the wood had been cleverly carved into overlapping scales until it melted into the prow.

No voices spoke, no hands raised a farewell. Our training for the raid had begun.

We used the oars, as I learned to call them, to get us clear of the small bay. It took quite some time, as I often tangled mine with that of the man in front. Behind me I could hear others doing the same. I began to hate the sound of wood clattering on wood and the spray of ocean that would spout over the side and drench my head.

The lead Spear told us to use the thick board in front of us to plant our feet and to help us push back against the oar. After that he waited until we were in open water and the figures on the beach were tiny before he spoke again. He was an impressive figure, the only one of us standing and with his helmet still in place. He did not shout. Rather he strode up and down the length of the ship, speaking in a low voice, his frowning mask leaning in to each rower.

"Lift . . . Together . . . Breath for breath . . . Feet firm against the block . . . Watch the man in front of you . . . Your arms must be as one rower . . ." And repeated, endlessly, the warning, "There is no place for error on a raid—a simple slip could cost the life of your brother, the loss of thralls, or the boat itself, when the time comes."

I concentrated, trying to adjust to the uncomfortable seat and the awkwardness of the oar that seemed to have a will of its own. If it was frustrating for me, it must have been unbearable for the seasoned rowers seated among us.

"Teach it," the Spear's voice whispered at my ear. "Teach the oar that you are master and it is thrall. Feel the water move beneath you." They were strange words to hear coming from a Spear, and yet I could hear the power in them. My hands responded.

Sweat pouring down my face stung my cracked lips. It did not take long for me to feel that lifting the oar even one more time might cause me to fall over. My breathing came out in a wheeze hardly different from the creak of the wooden slats around me. My hands slipped on the polished handle and I often had to slide them back down the oar to keep them from shooting off the end. Just when I thought I could do no more, I felt the boat surge ahead as every oar dug into the water at the same moment, broke the surface, and rose again in perfect time. From the corners of my eyes I could see the arms and backs of the others moving with me as if they were part of my own chest, the boat responding to our every touch. Even the sound changed from a raucous splashing to a hiss like the wind, as the sea sped beneath our feet.

There was no mist this far from the shore, and the wind bathed my face and arms deliciously. Gulls dipped and dived, soaring with us as if we had earned the right to fly with them. Back and forth across the water we sped, shooting past the entrance of the small bay a dozen times. I no longer felt as tired as I had. We were drawing strength from one another and from the boat itself, skimming the water.

"Raise oars!" The command came with a shout and hand signal.

I glanced behind me and caught Thief's eye. His tunic was soaked—with seawater or sweat, I couldn't tell. There was a gleam on his face, his teeth shining in the late afternoon sun. I felt it too. We had made our ship into a living thing, moving through the water like a fish, and the smile of pride stuck on my face as fast as Thief's grin.

We stayed out until the sun fell to the horizon,

stopping only to break for water and food. As we pulled up onto the beach I slid the oar out and onto the floor of the ship along with the others. Blood spattered onto the old wood and I looked at my hands. They were blistered all over, the skin broken open near the base of my thumbs. Many days ago, as a Digger in the grasses, I would have sucked the wounds quickly to hide the weakness from any watching Spear. Now I wiped the blood proudly across my tunic. Marumuk would be pleased.

Thief and I were given the second watch that night. No master came with us as we climbed stealthily out to the rocks of the northeastern headland, although the occasional glint of metal in the woods told us that someone was standing near. The sun had long since disappeared and the stars filled the sky all the way to the horizon. Waves broke heavily on the beach, and as I faced the warm breeze I thought of Grassland, where the tall stalks lay under many strides of water at night, and tiny shards nestled among their roots. There would be no hands to pick them in the morning. At least none that I knew of.

Through stories and chants the Red Fists had spoken to us of distant lands, and of battles on land and sea.

Everything was connected to the shards. Thralls were stolen to dig the shiny stones, only to become Red Fists and finally Spears as they grew older. I had not seen any Onesies since the Separation. Had they been taken back to Grassland to work once again as Diggers? Soon there would be more to join them.

Sick with helplessness at the part I was about to play, I leaned toward Thief. His dark head searched the ocean. His tangled hair flowing down over the top of his cape gave him a strange silhouette against the blinking stars. Of all of us, he had grasped the Spear ways the fastest. It was almost as if turning into a Red Fist had given him something better to be than a thief.

Pippa's gentleness had stopped me from drowning him the first time we had met, and from walking away the second time, when he lay pinned to the ground by an Outside arrow. What would she think of him now? What would she think of me? I wriggled on the cool stone, shifting my gaze to the water, then back to Thief. Pippa could not have imagined the kinds of things they had made us do around the fire pit, nor what it took to become a Red Fist.

Days had blurred into one nightmare after another in the Grove. There was often only time to think about the weapon in my hands and the faceless foes in front of me. I had beaten one boy senseless with a training stick and almost killed another for taking my portion of food, until I had realized what I was doing. Thief had stayed my arm from shaking the remaining breath out of the boy while Marumuk and the masters watched with approval. That same boy had helped me load baskets for the ship the night we tried to escape from Grassland. What had happened to us?

But when the days of training were over and darkness silenced the Grove, it was Pippa who filled my thoughts. Many nights I fell asleep with tears leaking down the side of my face, guarded from the others by an arm flung over my eyes.

I wrapped my cape more tightly around my knees, forcing myself to keep watch for ships. It was good to have Thief beside me. I could not imagine being without him. I traced a blister on my hand. Wherever Pippa was she would be happy to know that at least the two of us had managed to stay together. But I doubted that she was any closer to becoming like a Spear woman than she had been the night they took her from the Grove.

Thief stiffened and my arm went to the weapon at my side. He pointed. Far out on the ocean a white blur pitched in the wind. I cupped my hands around my eyes to block out the stars. Moments later I shook my head. I made the sign for *bird*. He grinned and sat back down. Not long after, several gulls flew over our heads, making for the beach. Their wings tilted in the wind, then the birds sank quickly to the sand below.

The watch passed easily, and Hammoth and Rezah came to replace us. We showed an open palm before heading back to our sleeping places at the fire pit. Rezah looked nervous, and although we could not speak it was good to know that all of us were feeling the same things.

The next day we practiced the sailing again, working the oars and taking turns at the tiller, turning the ship and sails at faster speeds. My shoulders and arms ached so badly I wondered if I would be able to lift them again when it came time for the raid. But over the next twelve days of training, my muscles hardened and thick calluses formed on the palms of my hands. I could feel my strength grow every time we took up our oars.

At the fireside one night there was a mood among the leaders that made me uneasy. Thief kept his shoulder pressed against mine as he sipped from a steaming cup. Although the masters' eyes betrayed nothing, both of us could feel that something was about to happen. They were waiting for something. Or someone.

Thief and I were sent for more wood for the fire. When we returned everyone was standing. Marumuk was pointing to the ship, then down to the earth at his feet. He did not greet me and his mood was somber, focused on what he was doing. As I moved closer I could see that he had made scratches in the dirt, a drawing like the kind Pippa used to make on the floor of our cell. The others were nodding and occasionally pointing to the drawing. Although there was no speech, one thing was clear from the way they were communicating: The time for raiding had come.

9

I SHIFTED MY HEAD, TRYING TO get used to the cold metal of the helmet pressing against my cheek. It was not a frowning mask like the ones the Red Fists around me wore. The helmet was rounded at the top, with eye and nose guard meeting at the bridge. While it did not cover our faces completely like a Spear's mask, it could withstand many sword blows. I found myself trying to ease my fear by staring at Thief.

We were hiding at the end of a wood, staring at a single point of light across a field of churned earth. The light did not come from a flame, but was the reflection of the moon off a shell-chime a hundred strides away. The eerie tinkling seemed to add to the uneasiness I was feeling, so different from a few nights before.

For five days our two boats had sailed along the coast, leaving the bay of Grassland far behind. I could not help feeling excited when the mountain disappeared behind us. Even Pippa would have smiled had she seen me pulling my oar like a man, deeper into the world than we could have imagined. When our sails caught the wind we flew across the water. Again I felt the thrill of making the ship move.

Warmer wraps were handed out as the air grew cooler the farther we traveled north. On the fifth night we had landed along a rugged coast where the water surged incessantly, filling the air with salt spray. We pulled the boats up onto the shore in darkness and tied them with thick ropes looped over immovable stones. We left the oars in place, ready for a rapid departure. At the top of the bank the two ships' crews divided, one band heading to the left, where they disappeared into thick trees, and our own group continuing to move north.

Marumuk had led us swiftly under the cover of trees and predawn, stopping briefly to confer with the other masters over a hastily earth-drawn map. We stopped marching when the trees thinned out, settling down for the chilling wait until dawn. My breath clouded in front of my face and I poked at it constantly. We did not see the cold very often in Grassland.

I rested my hand on the hilt of my sword, inching the pommel loose without a sound and rubbing the cold metal of the blade, as I did before every fight in the Grove. It was not wood beneath my fingers this time, and the edge was sharp enough to cut when I pressed down. I leaned back against the rippled bark of the tree behind me, reviewing Marumuk's orders in my mind.

The raid was on a cluster of three farms, built close together so as to ward off attackers, yet spaced out enough for the comfort of three families. The last scout had reported at least nine men, with a possibility of another five or six present if the farmers had recently slaughtered any livestock for market and brought in extra help. Any others would probably be sleeping in one of the lofts.

Twelve children lived in the three homes—the purpose of our attack. Thief and I were to stay together, close behind Marumuk, until we entered the largest building, the one closest to the woods and farthest from the others. Four children had been seen going in and out and only

II3

three males slept there at night, along with the women. It was our job to take one child each, preferably boys, no one under the age of three summers. Marumuk would lead us in and stand guard. If a male entered at any time we were to attack quickly, then leave at first chance, making straight for the woods. Short swords were to be kept loose in scabbard, and daggers in one hand.

I squeezed my eyes shut. It was well that Pippa was not here. As it was, her voice continued to tug at my thoughts even in my most terrified moments. What would her words be, concerning the things I was about to do?

I stared at Thief and found him returning my gaze. In the dim light his eyes shone without expression. It was a look he had developed since the Separation. Back at the Grove, I often felt that while his arms wrestled and fought like the others, his heart had long since left.

His hands moved and I read the signs.

Your mate. My mate.

I chewed the inside of my cheek. Everything we did now was to keep the hope of seeing our mates again. Everything. I felt the edge of my blade for the twentieth time, then hastily thrust it back in its sheath. I released a slow breath. Thief squeezed my hand again before turning away to look at the farm.

I nudged him. *Bad*, I signed, careful to keep my hands so that only he could see. *All bad.*

No think, he signed furiously. *Do it!*

It was not long before Marumuk was beside me, his strong hand tugging at my shoulder. I rose slowly to follow, Thief slipping in behind us. Hammoth and Rezah appeared as well, followed by the remaining Red Fists. Seeing their drawn daggers, I quickly ripped mine out from my belt. Sweat made my face slide against the cold metal of the helmet and I panicked for a moment when it shifted, half-covering my sight. I shook my head to find the eyeholes again.

We were moving, heading across the fields with no more cover of trees. No animals grazed in the cool air, and the sky was still empty of birds. Like a swath of shadow chasing the retreating sun we were bringing doom to an unsuspecting quarry.

At the sight of a fence nearest the first dwelling Marumuk sent Thief ahead, tapping his shoulder and pointing. Arrows were our worst enemy out here in the open, but there was no real danger of that with surprise as our weapon. Thief stole across the yard with perfect ease, keeping his cape close to his sides.

There was a single, smaller structure that housed the animals, only twenty strides from the homes. An unpleasant odor had grown stronger as we approached, and a dull shuffling sounded inside as the animals sensed us near. I wondered what they looked like. I had seen only horses before, and those from a great distance when the Outside armies had sacked Grassland. Pippa had tried to draw them for me ages ago in our cell, but they came out looking like boulders with legs.

We followed one by one, Hammoth and Rezah directly behind me, until all of us pressed up against a wall at the rear of the cottage. A small door was the only obstacle in our way, the only separation from the children inside. The thatch of the roof stood out like a bird's nest over our head—I had never seen anything like it. The dwellings in the Spear village had been made of stone and wood. It seemed strange to see woven grass for a roof.

Marumuk stepped up to the door, his feet landing so lightly I could not hear them above the livestock. His blade was out, glinting dully in one hand while the other pressed down on the latch.

Rezah's eyes flashed white like the bellies of fish escaping from torchlight. Hammoth rested his hand on my shoulder to balance himself on the step below me. All of our eyes held fast on Marumuk. The breeze lifted the edge of his cape, billowing it around his shoulders and making the heavy material snap. A long branch of hearth smoke hung in the air above the thatch, twisted by the early wind before drifting far out over the fields. Marumuk remained frozen, his hand on the latch, waiting, listening. The shell-chime tinkled one more time above my master's head.

He was in.

Maker help us. What evil are we about to do?

Heart pounding, I followed Thief closely, slipping in the door and blending into the darkness of the home. I could sense the others around me, filling the space quickly as their shoulders rubbed mine. The last man closed the door behind us, leaving the latch off. There was no going back now.

It was warmer inside, the cool cut off the moment the door closed. The final embers of a fire glowed on a hearth nearby, giving strange light to an even stranger scene inside the room. A table and chairs took up most of the space, although children's playthings lay strewn about the hearth as they had been dropped. *Family. And what had Pippa called the playthings? Toys. Shapes of animals made of wood, a ball, and one object that looks something like a girl, with wool for hair . . . We should not be here.*

I gripped my dagger tighter and took strength from the breathing of the soldiers around me, as I had been trained.

The scouting party had not been inside before, so we did not know where the children would be sleeping. Marumuk found me amid the others and pushed my stubborn feet forward. Thief went ahead, soundlessly finding ways of moving without knocking into the things around us. The openness of the first room ended quickly, with a piece of cloth splitting the space in half.

Thief stepped past the cloth, then stopped so quickly just beyond it that I almost bumped into him. The sound of a squeaky snore whistled out. Tilting his head forward to listen for a moment, Thief lifted a hand in front of my face. Then he went forward, raising his knife slowly in the gloom, one arm pointing ahead of him, the other poised to strike. A wave of dizziness clouded my sight and I leaned toward the near wall to steady myself. My hand brushed an object, hard and round like the ball by the hearth. It moved at my touch. I watched it tumble just out of reach and heard it strike the floor.

The tall bodies behind me stiffened. Even the swish of their capes froze. Silence filled the emptiness. The object began to roll past my feet, its trailing sound echoing in the small chamber like a boulder coming down the side of a mountain. There was a quick intake of breath from one of the sleepers, followed momentarily by a gentle sigh. The rolling continued until all I could think of was to run through the room and stomp the wretched thing into silence. Before I moved, it struck a wall and the sound fizzled into quiet. Not a breath could be heard.

Marumuk's fingers pressed through my cape and dug into my shoulder. I stepped farther into the room, seeing past Thief for the first time. A small window allowed starlight to fill most of the space. Lying not more than two strides from where I stood, three sleeping forms rested against the far wall. Children. There were more playthings here, but I could not determine their shapes.

Please, please, run away, get away! my heart shouted to them. These little ones did not deserve the evils they would find in Grassland or the Grove. The Spear helmet and clothes on my body suddenly felt heavy beyond bearing. I longed to be far away, so far that the sleeping forms could rest until dawn awoke them.

Marumuk's shadow on the floor stirred my feet into action and my legs moved without my heart's permission. Shifting my dagger back to my belt, I began to crouch my way to the first cot. As my shadow swept over a child's sleeping face I caught a glimpse of long lashes and pursed lips. A girl. Thief was already reaching beside me for a child half the size of mine.

Now or not, I whispered in my head. *Pippa, forgive me.*

A hand that did not feel like my own reached down and covered the girl's mouth. Her eyes flew open. In their brightness I saw the reflection of a helmet loom over her. In that moment, in less than a heartbeat, I remembered the dark mask that had once leaned over me.

But fear of failing pushed me now, and the soldier I had become took over. I slid the coverings off the girl and gripped her around the waist. I managed to cut off her scream by thrusting her face into the folds of my cape. Hauling her to her feet, I whispered in her ear as we had been taught. "Peace. Peace. Settle, be still."

The words echoed in my head, words of a strange language, spoken hastily, words warning not to call out to my mother and father. My head pounded inside the helmet and I lurched sideways, fearing that I would faint. Rezah was suddenly beside me, setting me back on my feet, his arm holding me up.

I sucked in a breath and the pounding eased. The dizziness and its memories went away.

I nodded to Rezah and gripped my captive more tightly. She began to kick the moment she sensed I was trying to move her to the door. Something crashed. A loud ring of metal told me that the Spears had all drawn their swords.

"Shhh," I hissed at the girl. "Shut up! They will kill you—all of you. Do you know that?"

A man's voice called from the darkness. The girl

stopped struggling, to listen. The voice came again. Someone was getting up.

Marumuk's hand found the starlight. *Three, go.* Immediately three Red Fists broke away from us and moved around the cloth. I could hear the sounds of a struggle and then the clatter of hearth coals being scattered. I gasped. If fire broke out the thatch would burn faster than hair. The girl began to fight with me again, violently, and this time managed to get out a scream. Her voice landed on my ears as if she had struck me with a stick. I quickly found her mouth again and clamped my hand back over it. Thief had lifted his burden from the bed and was already slipping away. Growing flames cast light beyond the cloth and our shadows suddenly grew grotesquely taller.

A clash of weapons from the main room set my heart on fire and I pulled the girl with such ferocity she came up off her feet to hang squarely over my shoulder. More shouts came and I found myself desperately wanting a hand free so that I could reach my dagger. Rezah and Hammoth covered both my sides, their swords ready for an attack.

Thief suddenly slammed into me, and our captives' heads clashed together as we tumbled into the far wall.

Rezah landed on the floor with Hammoth on top of him. I looked hard in Thief's direction to see why he had almost knocked me down. A looming form stepped down from a loft almost lost in shadow.

The man was tall, as large as Marumuk, and the fists he held in front of him could have contained my entire face. Twenty or thirty summers of lifting heavy bales of grain had turned those hands into hammers. I could only imagine what their strength could do to a body. The growl erupting from him sounded more like a beast than a man. And he had a right to be enraged. We were stealing his children.

Marumuk was still turned away, looking toward the shouts, unaware of the danger behind him. The surge of anger coming from the man was so strong I remained pinned to the wall. The girl on my back went wild, kicking, screaming, and very aware that help was on its way.

The man's growl suddenly turned into a roar and Marumuk spun on his heels to face the source of it. Firelight glinted off his helmet. His sword aimed at his attacker's throat.

They met at the center of the room, slamming

together like two young whales bursting from the water and meeting in the air. The farmer caught Marumuk's sword hand before the weapon descended, and they grappled in the moonlight, each willing the other to fall. A moment later the sword crashed to the floor. The farmer bellowed, managed to break one hand free, and struck Marumuk in the head with the full force of his tree-trunk hands.

Marumuk staggered back, then dropped to one knee, his chinstrap broken and his mask hanging precariously. The farmer wasted no time and snatched up the fallen sword. He swung it once above his head, his own face a mask of fury, and brought it down. But Marumuk raised an arm, caught the farmer's wrist and deflected the blow so that it glanced off the top of his helmet. Yet even then he could not get back to his feet. The farmer began to raise the sword again.

From across the floor my master's eyes caught mine and held fast. It was under that same stare that I had lost myself as a Digger and become the one thing I had dreaded most. Yet it was also Marumuk who had chosen me, had kept me alive time after time at the center of the

Grove when the training had been fiercest. I stared past his sagging shoulders toward the other room, where bursts of light showed the way to freedom. Across the fields and ocean my beautiful Pippa waited, her face smiling, her peaceful voice calling out, *robes and kisses.*

"Pippa." Marumuk gasped the single word while straining to hold the deciding stroke back. In my heart I saw the Grove, with the ash blowing in the summer wind around the circle of stakes. Mine lay broken, with Pippa's lock of hair lying motionless beneath it.

I let the girl slide from my shoulder and in the same movement ripped the dagger from my belt. In three strides I reached them. As the farmer's downward swing began I gripped my hilt with both hands and plunged the blade into his side.

In a scream of pain and rage the man swung wide and the sword came down to cleave the floor, narrowly missing Marumuk's knee and slicing the corner of his cape. The farmer's great barreled chest slammed into my face and I was thrown back onto the floor. Marumuk struck right after me, his own dagger finding its mark at the belly. As the farmer swayed, his eyes fell on me, looking contorted in the dancing light. His gaze then swung to the boy in Thief's arms. A sob burst out of his dying mouth.

Then he fell with a crash onto his back, both weapons still firmly embedded in his body. The girl wept, staring from my blood-soaked hands to the dying man on the floor. I sat up slowly, tears blurring my vision.

"Shhh. Peace. Please," I heard myself begging the girl. I reached out toward her. "Shhh. Forgive. Forgive me, Pippa."

The girl spat at me and tried to kick me away. Marumuk stood up, leaned to remove the daggers from the farmer, then turned to me. He offered the dagger to me, pommel forward, then gave me his hand to haul me up. The girl continued to curse at me in her own language and I could hear Rezah trying to control her. The clash of weapons helped clear my head.

Thief stared at me, horrified, the child in his own arms firmly locked against his chest. *Get up*, his eyes pleaded.

I tilted my helmet and took the dagger. As our hands clasped and Marumuk lifted me to my feet I felt his strength, his confidence, his command of obedience flowing up my arm. His helmet was back in place again.

He motioned toward the girl and I took her again, using my skills in wrestling to swing her back over my shoulder. Thief scrambled to his feet, as did Hammoth and Rezah, and moved quickly to join us.

Flames flickered on the walls as we entered the large room again. The girl struggled just a little less, as she had to avoid striking her head against walls as we moved. Women were screaming. Hefting the girl to my other shoulder I stepped past the body of a man lying facedown, his back smeared with blood. Two Red Fists stood over him. Two women much older than Tia sat hunched in a corner, their hands pinned to their mouths, their eyes staring.

The girl's head bobbed against my neck as she tried to look. At the sight of the man she stopped struggling, going completely limp in my arms. I stumbled forward, trying to get a better hold on her.

Hoisting her higher so that her head hung over my back, I grasped her legs and tried to open the door, but my sword caught on something at my feet. A wave of panic washed over me. A boy, older than me, lay holding his stomach and staring blankly toward the roof. Little gasps came from his mouth; his face was the color of burning wax. My sword had caught in the hem of his nightshirt, but it was not what was causing his pain. Blood oozed out from between his fingers.

I fled, ripping my sword free, slamming through the half-open door so hard that something snapped in a spray of splinters. The dawn had erupted into madness. Animals were lowing their worry, and everywhere I looked people ran like ghosts through wisps of smoke. A grizzled face appeared suddenly right in front of me, waving a sharpened tool. Hammoth pushed the man aside with a single stroke before I could even change direction. I gasped and ran on.

The girl was getting heavier with every step. When I had first put her over my shoulder she felt lighter than Pippa. But after thirty strides and with the weight of my helmet and sword, I began to stumble. Rezah took my elbow and supported me, all the while waving his sword threateningly at any who came close. Strangely, my greatest worry was keeping the blood on my hands from getting all over the girl. I could not understand why I was worried about it, but I kept swiping at my cloak whenever I had the chance to clean my fingers.

When I reached the first fence I leaned against it, my chest heaving. There was no sign of Marumuk. Behind me swords clashed and people screamed. A burst of flame shot up from the home we had just left, lighting up frantic figures in the shadows. Hammoth and Rezah were shaking beside me and yet both held their ground, ready to fight any who approached.

Thief stumbled out of the smoke. Blood oozed from a gash on his bare arm and his cape had twisted askew on his neck. He had also thrown his child over his shoulder, but unlike mine, his continued to thrash with a strength beyond his size. Blood was everywhere—on my weapons, on my hands, on my hands . . . The girl remained quiet, and it was only then that I realized that she was not conscious.

Thief nodded to us and took a firmer hold on his captive. I wanted to say something, of the horror only steps away from us, but our training held me back. Instead, I stared into the disaster we had just caused—the burning coals had not taken long to do more damage than I had thought possible—and waited for Marumuk.

The settlement no longer looked anything like it had

from the trees. Some of the Red Fists must have set fire to the other homes as well. Smoke enveloped the thatch roofs and spurted wickedly from tears along the walls. The light of flames from inside the main dwelling turned the fighting figures of the courtyard into warring shadows as they grappled with one another. Worst of all, a woman's voice, wailing her grief into the air, rose above the clamor below. I wanted to thrust my hands over my ears. A blast of heat struck my face as one wall of the central home collapsed, engulfed in flame.

The girl stirred, trying to lift herself off my shoulder. She was not struggling, and I welcomed the rest, so I allowed her to slip down, but kept one arm tightly around her neck. She stood with her back against me, staring at the destruction of her home. In that strange moment the sun broke from the east, bringing light to the evil of the new day.

The girl's long hair bunched against my arms and again my heart leaped back in memory. I saw another woman standing alone in smoke as soldiers took her family. She too had called for me, crying my name, reaching for me across flames. She had fallen before I could reach her, and my captor had scooped me up and away. I never saw my mother again.

The girl shook from time to time and her knees buckled at the sight of an old woman stumbling blindly back into the fire. A sob broke from her lips and she made a feeble attempt at breaking away. My own teeth chattered incessantly. "I am sorry," I whispered to her in my own language. "I do not want to do these things . . ." Hammoth punched the side of my helmet as a warning to be quiet.

Finally, when I could stand it no longer, Marumuk burst through the cloud of gathering smoke, followed swiftly by the others. They paused briefly at the fence while we were counted, and for a moment I was surrounded by familiar capes and helmets. Then a bell clanged, ringing out an alarm from one of the dwellings down from us. The girl was snatched from my hands and carried between two Red Fists like a sack of sand. As much as I was relieved to be rid of the burden, I felt a strange reluctance at seeing her go. Her face, though darkly tanned, was not unlike the shape of Tia's, and it suddenly struck me that we had indeed traveled far to the north. The resemblance did nothing but speed the guilt that much faster toward my heart.

I kept my eye on the girl while we raced for the trees, only looking down from time to time to keep my sword from catching on the hillocks at our feet. Every few strides I glanced over my shoulder, waiting for the twang of a bow or the shout of pursuit. Behind us wood groaned as a dwelling collapsed and a blast of heat blew past us, pressing our capes to our backs.

As we approached the beach the second ship had already returned. Most of the Spears stood on the shore, weapons in hand. A cluster of children sat lashed together on the sand only strides from the breaking surf. Thief's boy and the girl I had taken were added to the group. As they tied her to the others, the girl's head turned. Despair filled her face and I knew from her stare that somehow she was asking me for mercy, for help of any kind. She had heard the uncertainty in my voice and recognized a weakness. It was well that Marumuk had not seen it.

Pippa . . .

Thief tugged at my cloak.

I tore my eyes away. Above the crash of the waves I

could just make out the clang of the bells continuing to ring far behind us. Hammoth, Rezah, and Thief took hold of the bow-rope and started to shift the boat back to the roaring waters. The prisoners were carried on shoulders and hoisted roughly into waiting hands aboard the boat. I waded deeper into the cold water, holding my sword above my head, until Marumuk's strong grip hauled me up. The sun broke through the trees to light up the flushed faces around me. The boat rose and dropped, as if anxious to be at sea, while I clung with the others to her heaving side. As we pulled farther from the beach, the faint ringing of the bells finally lessened. The first raid was over.

I faced the wind. If Marumuk's words were true, Pippa would be waiting when we returned. Only five days to Grassland, only five days to let the wind and water wash the blood from my hands.

IT STILL FELT STRANGE TO BE looking at Grassland from the Outside. Bones lay everywhere. Even the stained feet of the mountain gripping the white sand beneath it gleamed in the morning light. Most of the bones were gathered on the main path leading into the Mouth entrance where the fighting had been the fiercest. The sun glared from dozens of places, wherever armor stuck out from capes or clothes. Shading the brightness with my hand, I could just make out the tumble of sprawled figures now lying lifelessly on the rock. The arms and legs of skeletons lay tangled as they had fallen, still gripped in battle rage.

In the distance, past the many rows of golden grasses, the sea was making its way back to the horizon, the sound of its leaving echoing off the cliffs of the two headlands that reached out into the bay. Above us seabirds swooped, nervously checking their flight and clattering their disapproval.

A low whistle made me turn my head. Thief was staring, taking in the scene for the first time since our long-ago escape. I looked at the others. Four of us lay on our stomachs, elbow to elbow, peering over the edge of the mountain's spine and down into the place that had been our world. A little farther along the trail, the new Onesies rested against the mountain's back, their faces downcast and weary.

Pippa had always said she could remember a time when she was not in Grassland, when there was a different place to live, with a Mother and a Father. I remembered little of the four or five summers before I was brought here. In my thoughts all I could see were the fields, the golden stalks where we had worked day after day under the watchful eyes of the Spears.

I rubbed my fingers. Even after the escape my skin was rough from eight summers of digging the shiny black shards. Grassland was a place of wealth beyond reckoning, and only after its destruction had we come to know it. To passing ships our mountain must have seemed like any other, a grinning skull of earth laughing into an enormous bay. They could not know that inside its stone was a maze of hidden tunnels leading to cages and cells that had been our home most of my life. And then the Outside had come, almost wiping out the Spears and nearly destroying us along with them, then leaving as quickly as they had come, their wagons filled with shards. Now only the birds and beetles were busy.

Staring past the grim scene below and out to the ocean ahead, I let the salt breeze tease my face, trying to forget about the evils we had just done. Marumuk had praised us for our obedience and success on the raid, and I reminded myself that if I had not followed orders, Pippa would be dead by now, and I with her.

I closed my eyes. Despite the hope of seeing Pippa, I was not anxious to go down among the bones. Yet even more than the dead, I feared what Pippa would see if she were able to pierce my defenses and discover what had happened in the last days.

Fourteen. It was a number that flicked and flitted

around my head like the flies buzzing at our faces. Fourteen lives were stolen in the course of five days of raiding, and for Marumuk it was enough. Enough to allow us to see our mates again.

Thief leaned against me.

Go now, he signaled. We stood slowly, walking along a path so narrow that if it had not been shown to us we would never have found our way over the mountain. At the bottom we were to enter the Mouth and head for the upper caves where, Marumuk assured us, our cellmates were waiting. Even now, spread out among the hills, the rest of the raiders remained in hiding, watching our slow procession make its way into the heart of Grassland. They would return to the Grove now and continue with the training of those who had remained behind.

At the bottom the path widened and I stood to the side of our line to allow our captives—the Onesies—to pass. I kept my sword drawn, visible for them to see, although from the weary shuffle of their feet I doubted there would be any trouble.

As the last of the children passed, the girl I had stolen cast her eyes at me again. Her hair was matted with sweat and tear lines stained her cheeks. With the others watching there was no way I could let her know the pain I was feeling over what I had done. But I thought that she could sense something, that I felt differently from the masters. And once, in the boat on the way home, my helmet had been knocked off when the sail was turned. The girl had stared at my guilt-ridden face, studying every feature before the helm was back in place. A trace of a smile had flickered at her lips before she looked back to her chains.

She could not understand that I had taken part in the raid to save my mate. I clenched my sword as she stumbled past. But would my actions be worth it? How would Pippa receive the news when she discovered what I had done at the farm?

Thief reached the first of the lifeless warriors. Without pausing we passed them, keeping a wide berth of their stiff arms reaching eternally for unseen foes. These and all the rest who lay on the slopes or openings to the mountain would be left untouched, to make any Outside armies think all the Spears were dead. Inside the mountain, Marumuk had said, all was different.

Standing in front of the Mouth sent shivers down

my back. The last time I had stood in this place, Thief and I were the only ones left alive in the empty fields of Grassland. The tall stalks stared back from the furrows, bowing in the afternoon wind as if they recognized Diggers when they saw them. Clusters of unpicked shards stuck up from the grassy roots and the sight of them sent an ache through my fingertips.

Rezah tapped my arm. I pulled away from the golden fields to step into the darkness of the Mouth. There was no need for either a guide or light in that place we had traveled for so many years, and yet to our surprise we found both. Torches lit the tunnel of the Neck as if there had never been a war, as if Outside had never come and the Twosies still lay silently in their cages. Standing at attention no more than ten strides inside, two Spears watched us approach. Both were large, perhaps even as big as Marumuk, with helmets reaching near the tunnel ceiling. We returned salutes while the new slaves stood silently between us, heads bowed, awaiting their doom. I forced myself not to look at them, especially at the girl. How strange it must be to come to this place and see it for the first time, with no knowledge of what was to happen.

When I came as a Onesie I had walked up these same paths without the hope of even having Pippa as a cellmate. I was the only one my age stolen from my village. The others had become Threesies quickly and were taken away. It was a lonely cell for almost half a summer, before Pippa came to me. She had brought faith and light to my life. I could only wish the girl and her brother would find comfort in each other.

Maker go with you, I whispered beneath my helmet.

The Spears broke away from the wall, one of them taking the front of the line and the other picking up the rear. Together they marched the Onesies in the direction of the lower cages. There would be a First Cleansing in the night ahead. Not all of the fourteen would be alive by morning.

A sob caused me to look up and in that brief moment I linked eyes with the girl. Tears gleamed off her face and she held up her bonds toward me, her eyes pleading. But the shuffle of the Onesies' feet grew steadily quiet as they dipped out of sight into blackness.

Thief looked in my direction.

Move on! I signed angrily, turning away from the

captives. We followed the branch in the tunnel, taking the upper passage as Marumuk had told us. At the touch of the cold walls pressing in against us I shivered, my eyes closing briefly on the memory. The sound of booted feet had echoed a thousand times before in my thoughts, like the ocean waves never ceasing their attack on the beach. But there was no sound of any more Spears.

As we worked our way deeper into the heart of the mountain, past the empty caves of the Twosies, I began to have a confusion of thoughts. Perhaps it was being alone in the caves again without Spears that set my fears into action, but I suddenly wondered if Marumuk had led us astray. We had long since branched from any tunnel I had ever known as a Digger—or even with Thief on the night of our first escape. The echoes reminded me both of the terror of that night and the freedom from the Spears that had followed. We had never been alone before, other than brief turns of taking watch near the fires at the beach. A feeling of uncertainty crept up my back.

Doors opened before us with a simple click of a latch, so easy now that we had been given the secret ways of the Spears. Unlike the doors that held back the water between Cleansings, these opened at the top by sliding a knob on the last board to the right. The one thing I was certain of was that we were moving upward, in a series of switchbacks, slowed only by the occasional door. As we started up another switchback, Thief suddenly stopped and leaned his back against the wall. Twenty steps ahead moisture gleamed off the wood of the largest door we had come to yet.

In the torchlight it was easy enough to see his signing. *Stop. Danger?*

I turned back to look at Hammoth. Sweat gleamed from under his nose guard. He shrugged.

It did not take much to realize we were all wondering the same thing. Rezah had already drawn his sword, glancing behind us nervously at the way we had come. In our memories the tunnels had never been a safe place.

Thief looked at all three of us in turn. "I do not like the silence."

I could tell by the lines around Hammoth's mouth that he was as shocked as I was at hearing Thief speak outside the Grove. But I was glad he had done it. I looked over his shoulder, trying to see the large door.

"What if we are attacked?" After so much silence, the words stuck on my tongue before spilling out into the tunnel and echoing off the stone walls.

Rezah shifted his position uneasily.

Hammoth stared. "Why would they train us to be Red Fists and then attack us? There is no sense to that. Coriko, you have shards in your head."

"Do *you* trust them?" I spat back. "Do you trust the Red Fists, Hammoth?"

He glowered, straightening to his full height. "You would be beaten for that kind of talk at the Grove," he said quietly. "Or anywhere else if they found out." His tone was ominous. "But I did not kill the farmer to save a Spear. You did."

Words froze on my lips as I stared at the angry eyes behind the helmet. A shiver rippled down my back. "The Spears would have killed Pippa if I did not do anything. You know that."

Thief stepped between us. "Peace, Hammoth. I trust Marumuk," he whispered. "And so do you."

"There will be trouble if we are caught talking!" Rezah's voice broke in.

Thief shook his head. "I do not think so. There were no commands about speech inside the mountain. This is a place of power for the Spears. They must speak away from the cells."

I had cooled down a little from Hammoth's words. "Marumuk is lord of the Grove, this much we know. But who is lord of the mountain? Nothing was said to me about this."

"The guards at the Mouth saluted us. They honored our capes," Thief said. "But why is no one here?"

Hammoth nodded. "We are all one. There is strength in stone, and two are better than one."

There was silence between us. In the quiet every breath, every shuffle of our garments could be heard. "We?" I lifted my eyebrows.

"Let us go forward, then," Hammoth whispered. "Slowly, swords out." He made to go past me.

"Wait." I laid a hand on his sword arm. "Pledge first."

"To whom? Marumuk is not here, nor is my master."

I continued to hold his arm. "Then to me, and Thief and Rezah. We do not know who is behind that door."

"You are a fool, Coriko," he spat. "Only my mate is behind there. And I want to see her."

"Pledge," I whispered again.

Rezah took a step toward us, sweat glistening off his clenched sword hand. "I will pledge."

"You are a fool as well, Rezah," Hammoth sneered. He raised his sword. "I am a Red Fist. This is our mountain and I will go forward without any more words of treachery. You would all be wise to do the same."

Despite my anger I could not have wanted a better fighter walking behind me. Between Hammoth and Thief I was much safer than Rezah, who walked alone at the rear. As we approached the door we slowed to a crawl, listening for anything that might tell us what was behind it. Thief reached for the latch. Swords drawn, we stood in attack position, one close behind the other. Even Hammoth's breath came quickly despite his talk of confidence in the Spears.

The door did not open. Thief tried again, pressing a little more firmly. The sound of a key turning in the lock from the other side made each of us press close against the others.

"Together!" I hissed. "Stand together!"

The door swung open and light poured out of the room, beaming on us as if we had stepped outside into bright sunshine.

"Put your swords away," a voice commanded. Marumuk stepped into the passage, his tall form casting a shadow over our faces. His helmet was off, as was the rest of his armor, with only the black cape swirling at his sides. "Enter quickly. This door is never kept open long."

We stood gaping, our weapons still poised for action.

"Come in," he said again. "Now!"

I stepped ahead of Thief and lowered my sword, trying hard not to look into my master's maskless face. The brightness of the room came from holes in the ceiling and walls, like the windows we had seen in the Spear village so long ago. But these were more cleverly crafted, carefully cut through the thickness of the mountain to let in light. The floor was made of stone, like the tunnels, and against the far wall were weapons of various kinds resting against a wooden structure. Large tables took up most of the space, with benches—much like the ones on the boats—for sitting. There were numerous other things around us that

I did not recognize, but it seemed to me in that moment that we were standing in a resting area of some kind.

I blinked, staring around me dumbly at the vast, sun-filled room. I sheathed my sword and gave Marumuk my attention. "We did not expect—" I started.

He waved my words away. "Of course you did not *expect*. You were being tested. You are always being tested until you no longer wear a Red Fist on your chest. Remember that."

I did not know what he wanted me to say, so I stood silently, watching his every movement.

"Take off your capes and training clothes. There is hot water for washing in the buckets." He pointed behind us, where four large buckets sat steaming in the sunlight. "Clean yourselves well, then put on the garments laid out for you on the table. I doubt your mates will want to smell you the way you are now."

At the mention of mates, a wave of weakness spread through my knees.

"They are waiting for you in the hall of meeting." Then he turned and walked toward a door to our right. As his hand struck the latch he turned back to me, his fierce eyes and muscled neck looking as frightening as the day I had first met him. "Well done, Coriko. I do not easily forget when a man saves my life." He left without another word.

None of us spoke for a moment. Then Hammoth broke the quiet of the room. "Idiot," he whispered at me. "Does this look like an attack? New clothes and hot water? You are a fool."

I continued to stare at the door my master had left through, choosing to leave Hammoth's words alone for the moment.

"Maybe so, Hammoth," Thief said. "But that makes him his master's fool. Do you think it is wise to suggest that Marumuk chose the wrong thrall?" He chuckled dangerously. "I wonder what Marumuk would say to that."

Rezah ignored all of us and hurried over to the buckets of water. Faster than I thought possible he removed his outer gear and plunged his head into the bucket. When he came back up his hair was steaming, and water ran into his smiling mouth. It was something Bran would have so easily done. I had not thought of my friend for some time, and the sight of Rezah looking like a fool made my heart ache at the loss again. If becoming a Red Fist had not made me feel close to Rezah, certainly his resemblance to Bran made up for it.

The clothes they had put out for us were not any kind of Spear garment that I had seen before, and they were clean, folded neatly in separate piles.

It took a while, but in time all four of us stood staring at one another, bodies clean and clothes in place. I had washed my hands many times but still they did not feel clean.

"There is nothing on your hands, Coreeko," Thief said. "But you smell strange." He sniffed at me.

I raised my arms to look at the cloth. "I am clean." I tapped Thief's shoulder. "You do not smell at all," I answered. "It is a good change."

He shrugged. "Pippa will not recognize you, I think. You have grown taller, and the garments make you look bigger than you are."

"I wish for my cape and sword," Hammoth announced. "These are not the clothes of a warrior."

His words echoed in the large room. Thief gave me a

fleeting glance. It was dangerous to show what we truly felt around him, so caution was necessary.

"I would like to go now." Rezah stared at the door.

"And I as well," I agreed. The other two nodded.

Stepping through the door Marumuk had shown us took almost as much courage as entering the room for the first time. My heart thumped as I searched for the hall of meeting over Thief's shoulder.

No more killing, Pippa's voice whispered in my head. *No more killing. We must not be like the Spears.*

I clenched my fists, staring down briefly at my hands. This tunnel went on for a way before ending suddenly at another large door.

Thief stopped. He leaned his head against the wood. "There is whispering on the other side. Female."

"Open it!" Rezah hissed.

"What if she is not there?" I gasped.

"Of course she is," Hammoth growled. "Marumuk said our mates were here."

Thief reached down for the latch. "Now we find the truth."

The chamber was huge, far larger than the room with

steaming buckets, and it was full of girls everywhere I looked. Sunlight streaming in from the ceiling reflected off beautiful white robes and clean, shining faces. Not a single Spear could be seen. There was an intake of breath as they searched our faces, quickly followed by long sighs of disappointment at the sight of only four of us. Feelah suddenly appeared from nowhere, gripping Thief around the waist before he could respond, and trying to lift him off his feet. There was a burst of laughter from those near him, but I did not wait to watch, for above the crowd I heard a voice, ringing clear, and saw a flash of bright hair.

The girls in front of me parted.

For the briefest moment the walls of the room disappeared and I stood as I had many days before on the moonlit beach outside the Spear village. Pippa's hair was braided, with one strand on the sides, but the rest had not yet grown back. A red flower looked out from behind her ear.

"I fixed my dress," Pippa said quietly. Of all the white clothes in the chamber, hers was the only one with color, the colors of sky and sea and sunsets. It was impossible to count the number of times I had waited for this moment, yet as she stood before me my feet would not move and words froze on my tongue. She did not wait for me. The dress of many colors flowed forward and suddenly I was holding Pippa so tightly I could hear the breath squeeze out of her.

Tears worked their way down my cheeks, falling to land on her shoulder. My hands found each other at the small of her back and I resisted the urge to wring them. I held them away from her so that they would not stain her dress.

She tried to draw back to look at my face, but I was unable to meet her eyes just yet, and kept her close to my chest. Her arms tightened around my neck and I could feel her cheek sliding up to mine. She gave a little shudder.

"You have seen many things while you were gone," she whispered.

"Yes."

"You have *done* many things as well."

"Yes." I hardly heard my own whisper.

"Let me look at you."

"No."

She reached behind her and touched my hand. Then

she spoke purposefully, each word searching my heart as if I were speaking myself. "And you are afraid of the things you have done."

My voice cracked. "Yes."

She held me for the longest time, her head now pressed to my cheek, as if listening to the story within my thoughts. Then I felt her pulling away a little. "Come with me. Let us go where we can speak more easily."

I resisted. "What about Thief and Feelah? And where is Tia?"

"Come with me, Corki."

The crowd around us smiled and laughed, but a sickness grew in my stomach as I followed my mate farther into the chamber.

II

WE WERE ALONE. PIPPA TOOK my hand and walked us away from the others, through an empty hallway to a small sleeping chamber not far from the hall of meeting. I fell exhausted onto one of several beds of straw neatly covered with blankets.

"Feelah will be along soon with Thief," she said quietly. She knelt beside me with her beautiful hair glinting in the candle's light. "I have asked her to give us a little time so that we may speak in the Northern tongue."

I listened to every tone in her voice, hoping, yearning that she would somehow understand the things I would have to tell her. "I worried about you," I said, touching her nose with my finger. "Every day, every night, I worried."

She nodded. "I know."

There was a scuff of footsteps, followed by soft laughter, as several girls walked past our chamber.

"Where is Tia?" I asked. "And why are there no Spears?"

"I will tell you soon." She fixed her gaze on my hands. "It was difficult for you, I think," she said. "The Spear ways are not easy for males."

I leaned up on one elbow. "It was not good, Pippa. The things that happened, the things they made us do . . ."

After so many days of being without her, I felt an awkwardness I had never experienced before.

"Speak now and tell me everything that happened."

"I cannot seem to remember anything."

She brushed the hair off my forehead. "Go back to the Grove. Think of the night we were Separated."

"I do not want to think of those things. I just got here. I want to sit with you and talk is if we were back in our cell and none of this had ever happened."

"That is not what is truly in your heart. You do not want to go back. And it is important for you to tell me everything, Corki."

"Why?"

"I will explain later. The others will be here soon and we have little time for me to think."

There were so many things I wanted to ask, and many other things I had kept secret for so many days that I needed to speak them. I stared at my cellmate. While one hand stroked my hair, her other tapped the ground absently.

I closed my eyes and began telling the story that had filled my days with darkness from the night she had been taken from me, leaving out nothing except the attack on the farm. From time to time she winced at the words, and at one point drew her fingers to her mouth in surprise.

"So much pain," she whispered. "How terrible."

Guilt lay tight in my throat, gripping my heart and turning the warm air of the chamber cold. I looked away from her. "Other things happened too."

"What things?"

I sat up, suddenly angry. "What does it matter? We have not seen each other in over a hundred days and all you want to know is the bad things. Why can you not just let them be forgotten? It is for the best. We are together, here in this place."

"*Here in this place*," she repeated. "And for how long? Did Marumuk tell you?"

My mouth fell open. "How do you know Marumuk?"

"He comes to the hall of meeting often. There is no time to speak of that now. Did he say when you would return to the Grove?"

"No."

"So you may have to leave tomorrow for perhaps another hundred days? Or even longer."

"I do not know. I have not thought about it. I was so happy to see you—"

She leaned forward quickly and took both my hands in her own. "Listen to me, Corki." Her eyes flashed. "They treat us well here. We are given the best food, a common language, clean clothes. New skills are taught every day, with plenty of time in between for braiding and laughing." She spoke as if she were spitting out a mouthful of saltwater. "It is so pleasant that many of the girls have stopped talking about leaving. They spend their days picking fresh flowers for their hair and dreaming of the peaceful times they will have when their mates return."

I thought of the white-clothed group we had been with earlier, and imagined them sitting beside cool, flowing water, smiling and talking. It was not difficult to believe.

Pippa went on. "The peacefulness we have been given has become so strong that no one speaks about escape anymore without frowns appearing. I no longer trust anyone but Tia and Feelah. And even they have felt the power of this place," she added. "It is getting harder to leave. There are good people here."

She squeezed my hands. "My heart has told me from the beginning that all of you were in danger, that White Eye's words were true."

I nodded, trying to find a way of telling her. Nothing seemed to fit, so I let the words tumble.

"White Eye spoke the truth. Everything he said came true." My chin dropped to my chest. "I killed a Father." The light of her candle blew out with my breath and I was thankful for the darkness at that moment.

Her hands went limp. "What did you say?"

I continued miserably. "He . . . he was protecting his children as we raided their farm . . . He was going to kill Marumuk—and if he had, I would never see you again.

So I stuck a dagger into his side. He died while I stole his daughter from him." I could not look at her face. "I did not want to do this deed, Pippa. His blood will not come off my hands, nor the sadness of his daughter's face leave my thoughts."

She did not speak for some time, and I felt the weight of silence settling on my shoulders. Her body trembled, sending shudders down her arms. When her hands pulled away from mine, it was too much for me to bear. "Pippa, I beg you, do not leave me for doing these things. Do not hate me. Every day I hate myself for the evil that is on my hands. If you leave me now, how could I ever come back here again? It would have been better to die in the Grove."

Although I could not see her face I sensed the battle going on inside her. I had spent years in the darkness of our cell knowing every murmur, every breath that she took. The sounds she made now spoke of uncertainty, fear, and terrible loss. I wanted desperately to take her in my arms, and yet with one stroke I had lost my right to do so. The small space between us now seemed as huge as when I had been at the Grove, not even knowing where Pippa was.

"Do you want me to leave?" The words came out of my mouth like a stranger's, someone who did not know my beautiful Pippa. My shoulders felt heavier than when they were weighed down with a cape and helmet. I could not make myself stand.

The sound of a flint being struck stirred me and I lifted my head. The candle was alight once more, revealing Pippa's tear-stained face. When she finally spoke, her voice was on the edge of a cry, held steady by only the fervor of her words.

"The blood that you have shed is on my hands as well. For you and I are one in heart. What you have done, I have done as well."

I threw my arms around her and in one motion lifted her off her feet and hugged her, as if pulling her from the edge of a cliff. She clung to me, hope flowing between us as light to a new day. Tears came quickly. I did not brush them aside as I would have in the Grove or in the caves.

"I fear we must leave soon, Corki," she whispered. "For every heartbeat that we stay in this place, with every child stolen and every parent killed, the stains of our guilt will grow. Every one of us who grows to be the mother of a Spear is no less at fault than those who are forced to carry a sword."

"Thank you, Pippa," I whispered.

She smiled. "But now we must think of what we will do next."

I eased her down and we sat side by side on the edge of the cot. While I basked in relief at her forgiveness, she was already working her thoughts into words. "Were the Onesies brought here to the cells?"

"Yes. We took them through the Mouth and left them with guards. They will be taken to the lower cages, I think, for the First Cleansing."

"Hmmm. That might be the most difficult part."

I looked at her. "What part?"

"Getting them out of the cages."

"What is your thinking?"

"Escaping, of course!"

I shook my head. "This is not an easy thing, Pippa."

"No, but—"

"Shhh!" I hissed. "Listen."

Steps outside. Then the cloth was swept aside and Feelah entered with a candle, followed closely by Thief. It was too soon. Pippa and I still had much to say.

"Coriko!" Feelah threw an arm around my shoulders. "I am so happy at the sight of you!" She used the Spear speech and I could not help smiling at her. It was going to take a while getting used to speaking so easily with everyone. Thief eyed the walls, looking for doors, windows—any way out of the chamber if we needed it. It had become so natural for us to do that it did not matter if we were in the center of the Spear kingdom.

"What do you think of all this?" he grunted. His eyes roved to Feelah, to Pippa, then back to me.

"I do not know what to think yet. Pippa has told me only a little."

"We are together again!" said Feelah.

"Please sit down," Pippa whispered.

Feelah's smile disappeared. "Pippa, what are you afraid of?"

"Of everything we have feared together, Feelah. Everything. Please sit, then I will explain."

All of us sat on the floor this time, close enough that our knees were touching.

"Do you not understand what is happening here?" Pippa asked. "Can you not see what they are trying to do?"

None of us spoke.

She continued. "This is how they keep us. Forever. This place is how our names join all the others on the stones in the graveyard outside the Spear village."

"What are you talking about?" Thief spoke for both of us.

"Do you remember White Eye? Do you remember the Spear village and the gravestones we saw just beyond it?"

"Of course," I said.

"Now it is happening to us. Look at us! The girls have everything they want here, with the promise of gaining even more if we follow the rules and obey. We have been taken to the village, where already homes are being rebuilt and the old ways are being practiced again. Each of us has been promised a new home, to live in peace, to be with our mates and have more than we have ever had before."

A splinter of hope began to grow inside me. I remembered the village well, although it had been a long time since I had seen it. Even destroyed, it had seemed beautiful to me, with its colored cloth and sharply cut stones.

"Our own home!" I almost sang the words.

"You see?" she answered. "Do you feel the hope rising inside?"

"Yes."

Pippa took a deep breath, as if she had been holding all these thoughts inside for so long that she knew them as well as we knew our swords.

"That is what the Spears want. And so the boys lose their hearts to become Spears, under the threat of losing us if they do not obey. While the girls fall deeper into the dream of false freedom."

"Pippa—" Thief began.

"Here it must stop." Pippa slapped the floor. "We at least have each other, our own mates together in one place, while the others can only wait in hope. Is it not laid upon us to go as the very first who have been given the chance?" She reached out to Thief. "We did not run from Grassland to become thieves of children. We escaped to be free and find a new way."

My friend said nothing.

Feelah spoke. "We ran from Grassland because we had to. We hid in the stream-trees because the Spear village was burning and we did not know when soldiers might return. If we run again, something worse may happen. You and I have spoken of this before. At least my Thief is alive, and your Coriko is here, even though we feared the worst. Why should we run?"

I turned to my cellmate, thoughts warring within my own heart.

Pippa sighed. "Because it is not who we are. We are not Spear women." She stared at me. "And you are not a Red Fist." Her gaze shifted to Thief. "Neither are you. Not here." She touched her heart. "It may be that for a little while we have had to live and breathe the same air as the Spears, but it is not who we must be. And we have the choice here and now to change our path."

"Then what do you say we should do?" Feelah asked.

"I say we leave before Marumuk takes the boys away again. We cannot risk the chance of having them leave for the Grove and be gone for another hundred days. We must escape. Tonight."

"There is still a little time, I think," Feelah said. "These boys have been trained. This is where they are to serve one day. Would not Marumuk show it to them, as he did to us, before they return to the Grove? And we have been given leave of our duties in the hall for as long as the boys are here. There has been no talk among the old ones of the boys leaving again."

Pippa shook her head. "I do not know. But my heart would be more at ease if we all agreed to leave together."

"We will go with you, Pippa," Feelah said. "We always have."

A long silence filled the chamber.

"What does Tia say?" I asked. "And why is she not here?"

My cellmate glanced at Feelah. "I will speak to Coriko in our own language for a moment, where there are more words that we know." She turned to me. "Many things have happened while you have been gone."

"What is wrong with Tia?" I whispered.

"Nothing is wrong. But her heart is confused."

"That makes no sense to me. What is she confused about, and why would she not be here to lead us as she always has?"

"She has love for Marumuk."

The words struck me like an unseen fist to my head.

Pippa continued. "I told you that Marumuk came here often. There are two reasons. The first is that he comes to make sure that defenses are strong should Outside ever return, and to visit the village to see that the rebuilding goes unhindered. The next part will be harder for you to hear." She drew in a breath. "When we arrived at the hall of meeting after the Separation, we were guarded by Red Fists for two days. But they were not harsh with us and there was more freedom than we had experienced before. Tia tried several times to find ways to escape. She was still in great despair over Bran and did not seem to care about living or dying. Marumuk took her away from us and we did not see her for many days. I feared the worst."

I held my breath.

"Instead of harming her, as I had thought, Marumuk spent time with her, teaching her the history of the Spears and walking in the open air. His own mate was killed when the Spear village was destroyed, and Tia felt a tenderness beginning to grow in her heart for him."

My head swirled. It was impossible to imagine my master speaking soft words and being kind to Tia.

"When she returned, we had already been given new chambers and clothes and food, as well as the company of older Spear women who had not been killed in the attack from Outside. Tia was different when she came back. The emptiness had left her eyes."

"Has she become a *Spear*, then?" The words were difficult to say.

"No. There is still a desire in her to leave, I think." Pippa frowned. "Or . . . perhaps it is not so much that she wishes to leave, as it is to change the way things are here. I do not know—it is difficult to understand her thinking recently. But her heart is in turmoil. She will be here before long. She sleeps in this chamber." She nodded to the cot beside me.

"Will she come with us, then?"

"I do not know. Perhaps she may."

Feelah had been speaking with Thief, and as Pippa finished we turned to each other and spoke in the Spear tongue again. He stared at me gravely. "I do not like it when Tia is not here. She is good. She is smart."

"Pippa says she might come with us."

He grunted. "We must know who is with us and who is not. I do not want an arrow in my back because someone keeps turning around to look at the way we came. The Spears show no mercy for those who run away."

Pippa leaned toward him. "Then think carefully, each one, for we may not be given another chance."

"How will we leave?" Thief's voice was louder than I liked.

Pippa's answer was much more guarded. "For that, we must wait for Tia." She blew the candle out.

A long while later, as we sat whispering, the patter of bare feet could be heard in the tunnel. I crept forward and poked my head out beyond the hanging cloth. A single candle flickered its way toward me and the outline of Tia's long hair gleamed back at me.

"She comes!" I hissed over my shoulder. I shuffled back into my place between Pippa and Thief. The curtain moved aside and our Threesie stepped into the room. I gasped, for Tia looked more like a Foursie than I could ever have imagined. Her hair was unbraided, but not tucked back the way the girls held theirs behind their heads. Instead it flowed around a keener, wiser face, and down over her shoulders. Her dress was the same as the others, but she filled it like a woman and not like my Pippa. My thoughts went immediately to the Mother we had found in the Spear Village so long ago.

"Peace, Coriko, Thief," she held out her hands to us. She spoke the Northern tongue, which surprised me.

We took her arms and she drew us closer. "My brave boys." She kissed the top of my head. I felt awkward and pulled back to look at her face.

"Look at you!" she whispered. "You have more muscles, and your eyes look back at me as though both of you could handle an army of Strays. I would not doubt it."

"Where have you been?" I finally managed. "We needed you and you were not here."

She switched into the Spear language, speaking slowly, with words that took time to understand. "Many things have changed, Coriko. We find ourselves in a new place once again, and yet together."

She spoke the tongue with practiced ease. The sound

of it coming from her mouth hurt me more than when Pippa had first used it.

"What strange ways our paths have led," she went on. "Danger, death, friendship . . . sorrow." I knew she was thinking of her brother. "I have walked down so many of them that it is hard to know which one I belong to anymore." Her voice faltered a moment and I glimpsed the old Tia.

"My path has never changed," I answered. Yet even as I spoke I could feel the splash of blood on my fingers and the urge to wring my hands. My words were trembling, but I spoke them for Pippa's sake. "Nor has Thief's. We know our way. And so should you."

She smiled. "Is that so?"

Her warmth was still there, and yet I found myself pulling away from her to sit back beside the girls.

"Have you not learned anything these last days?" she asked. "Anything that is good?"

"I have learned how to kill better," I answered. Pippa took my hand.

Tia's smile faded. "Have you not been trained to protect yourselves and others? Have you not been given the tools to keep that which is most important? Are you not sitting beside your mate without the fear of being struck by a Stray's rock? Does she not look more beautiful than ever before?"

Pippa did not say anything and I wondered if this conversation had taken place within these walls before.

I lifted my hands up in front of Tia. "Blood is on these hands, even if you cannot see it. I cannot get it off. In Grassland I fought to save Pippa, as many times as there are stones on the beach. But never did I sneak into a house at night to steal a child and kill a Father."

Her eyes squeezed shut for a moment. When they opened, tears slipped out to fall on my open palms. "Good and bad live together," she said. "I have discovered this much. Nowhere is there only good." She glanced at my cellmate. "I wish Pippa were right. I wish we could find a home or make our own where we could live in peace, but there is none. Each place has its Strays and its Spears."

"How could being a Spear ever help me?" I growled.

She sighed. "Can you not see that it is because I am wearing this dress and not a work-cloth that I know you will not return to the Grove for two more nights? I know the secret tunnels of the mountain—the paths that are seldom taken and least watched. I know enough to help you to escape."

She continued. "I know that Marumuk does not have enough guards to keep all the tunnels watched. Because you are wearing the Spear tunic, you are allowed to walk freely in the tunnels and so find your way out of the mountain at night, by a way I will show you. You will leave this place in search of another—nothing I say will stop that." She smiled sadly. "And yet, if I wanted, truly wanted, I could speak one word and the four of you would remain here forever. Do you see? Good and bad together."

I put my hands on either side of her face and looked deeply into her brown eyes. "Where is Tia?" I whispered.

Her voice broke. "I do not know, Coriko. I think here, but I do not know anymore."

Pippa leaned forward. "Will you come with us? Your family, Tia, think of them. We could find them. Your village, your old life."

"When I came to Grassland," Tia answered, "you showed me a new family and the hope of finding my way back to the north. That dream, and my brother, were taken from me by the Strays. Now I face another choice. Power is being given to me here, Pippa. Power to make changes. If you stayed, I believe we could turn the path of the Spears for the good."

Then she looked at me, and spoke in the Northern tongue. "Marumuk believes you will be a great leader among the Spears. He told me what happened during the raid. He thinks that in a few summers you would be ready to join him as a master. In time, and with Pippa's help, we might not even need to make raids anymore. We could build a new home here, Coriko. Strong and safe where our children could not be taken from us ever again."

No words came out. I stared helplessly at my cellmate, confusion falling on me like rain.

Pippa's gaze never faltered and she changed the language so that the others could understand. "A sword is always hungry, Tia. It is a restless creature that never ceases looking for more. How can we stay if there is even a chance that the boys will have to go on another raid? Will Feelah and I let them go, knowing that more children will be torn from grieving hands? That is a choice I will not make."

"Nor I," said Feelah.

Tia sighed. "As I thought. Then let us speak more of it in the daylight. Tomorrow Marumuk will take you to see the new village. Perhaps then your heart will change. But do not talk around the others," she warned. "Very few think as you do, and the laws are still kept."

I turned to Pippa. "Are there not other girls who would come?"

Pippa shook her head. "Would you leave your mate behind? No, it breaks my heart, but only those who can must go now. The others must try when their time comes and more mates are brought here. We can only hope that their hearts will not fail them and that they will try to do the same."

"When will we go?" Thief broke in. He eyed Tia suspiciously and I knew that, like me, he suffered great hurt by her words. Feelah laid a hand on his arm.

"I understand his doubt, Feelah," Tia said.

"Tomorrow night, if it is still your intent. I will lead you, that much I do know. Whether I come with you or not, the morning will have to show me." She lifted my chin. "I know it is hard for you, Coriko, but now you must trust me once again. It is dangerous to speak our plans. Do not talk of this again. At the right time you will know when to go. Just be ready. Much must be done and risked before it is time." She sighed again. "I wish Bran were here."

"Lie down," Pippa said softly. "I will comb your hair until you sleep." Tia lay down without hesitating and closed her eyes under my cellmate's touch.

In the awkward silence that followed the chamber fell into darkness, and we each lay down to sleep for the night. Soon Pippa nestled close to me. The smell of her hair sent a wave of peace to my heart. I could hear Thief snoring, a comfortable reminder of his strength. And yet it was not until long after the others slept that my eyes closed. For there was danger lurking in the tunnels around us—if not now, then soon, it would come.

I was not anxious to meet it.

12

THE SPEAR VILLAGE LOOKED nothing like the burning ruins we had discovered as a group of lost Diggers. The smoldering gates had been replaced by towering new beams, carefully cut and carved with skill. Inside, as Marumuk showed us, the building was progressing slowly, but with no less beauty than the entrance. Many Spears worked on the rooftops, and more were hammering from inside the dwellings all over the village.

"There will be enough for four hundred dwellings," he said with a sweep of his great hand. "And space at the forest edge for more." We stood gaping at the center, eight of us besides Marumuk and Tia. Outside of the mountain we had been told to wear our helmets and weapons again, and although it was hard for Pippa to look at me, I felt more at ease with a dagger in my belt. Rezah had joined us, and stared wide-eyed at the view. His surprise was still as obvious as my own. I would need to speak to him, at least, before our time came. Hammoth stood away, his mate at his side.

Thief and Feelah never moved farther than ten strides away from us. We had agreed that until we escaped that night we would all stay on alert, ready to flee if anything happened to change our plans. It nearly drove me mad that we knew so little of what Tia had in mind. Our lives lay in her hands, yet she had told us nothing of what she intended. To make things worse, as the day grew older the choosing of paths became more difficult. Even Feelah's decisiveness from the night before seemed to weaken at the sight of the beautiful buildings.

My master drew me aside from the others, as if to show me a dwelling. From behind his helmet his eyes pierced mine. "What do you see here?"

"I see a dwelling."

He stretched his arms wide. "Look at this place. A hundred Spears are working while another two hundred guard the mountain, the Grove, the desert, and the sea. We will never be taken again, Coriko. Our elders died because they could not foresee an army crossing the desert. But I have seen it. I stood with those who held the last tunnels."

Standing beside him in that place, I did not doubt that he had single-handedly kept the Spears alive.

"Never again will we be fooled or surprised, nor lose what we have made."

Behind him Pippa watched me carefully. My words counted twice as heavily now and I knew it. I spoke slowly, and with the same care I used when walking over barnacles at low tide. "There are still many Spears despite the war against Outside."

He nodded. "It was good fortune that so many were in the Grove being trained. If they had been at the mountain they would have been slaughtered with the rest. And there are tunnels deeper than Outside ever knew."

I did not answer. He put a hand on my shoulder and I almost leaped back in surprise. It was all I could do to concentrate on his words while his hand rested there. "Coriko, Tia speaks highly of you. I chose you because you helped lead a group of children out of the mountain almost without a scratch, and that under the nose of an invading army. You have trained well, better than the others and, like the Thief, you think for yourself. You have also proven yourself as a soldier, and shown that you can do your duty under difficult circumstances." His hand moved away and he actually patted my back before he continued. "There is a great place for you here. You, your mate, and the others." He nodded behind me. "Homes, power, men to stand under your command. These are the things I see for you."

"I am honored," I said quietly. There were times when I felt that his eyes could see inside me.

Over his shoulder a small figure, lifting bricks to waiting hands on the roof of a dwelling, turned at the sound of our voices. I stiffened. The girl I had stolen from the farm looked back at me out of a startled face. It was hardly the place I expected to see her. I had assumed she would have been kept at the mountain in the Onesies' cages. I barely caught Marumuk's next words.

"We will be returning to the Grove tomorrow night. From the start of the new moon, training will be complete in another hundred days. Then we will raid again. A larger raid, with more swords. With enough new Diggers we will be able to start harvesting shards again as well as build the army. I want you to be among those who do the training. You will be allowed to see your mate regularly. A home will be built for you. Riches from over the sea will come with trade ships and you will be clothed in colors."

I could not stop a picture—a picture of Pippa lifting colorful dresses in her arms—from entering my thinking, even while I looked back at the girl. "What will happen to those we have already taken?"

He waved his hand. "They were a part of your training. For now they are useful to help build the village. In time they will find a place among us."

An angry shout from the rooftop sent the girl scurrying off to find more bricks.

I watched as the back of her work-cloth disappeared around the corner of a dwelling. "Why did you stay, master, and not leave when Outside finally left this place?" If I could have caught the words before they left my mouth I would have, but it was too late.

Marumuk reached out to the wall in front of us and

poked at the mortar, scraping the brick and wood with his finger. "Do you know how long it takes make a dwelling?"

I shook my head.

"With four men we can have it standing with a roof by the end of one full day. Do you know how long it takes to burn one to the ground?"

His second question forced me to look at him closely.

"An attack in the morning will leave little standing by midday if done properly. An entire village finished. Life changed forever within half a day."

"Half a day," I repeated, not knowing what he was talking about.

"I lost everything I knew in half a day." His voice came out in a whisper, although I did not sense that he was trying to keep it hidden from anyone. "Would it not seem wise to make your pledge with those who can best keep it, and give you more than you can imagine as well?"

When I did not say anything he continued. "Until this day I have been your master and you have been my thrall. But when you leave the mountain again we will go as brothers. I will continue to show you the ways of war, but it will be with the knowledge that you have saved my life, just as I shall save yours in the battles to come."

"Yes," I mumbled, having nothing else to say. I wanted to find Thief or Pippa with my eyes, but I could not turn without causing insult.

"The way of the Spears is the strongest path there is." He clapped my shoulder again. His words sounded the same as Tia's, only with a lifetime of conviction behind them.

"But did the Spears not fall when Outside came?" I answered, uncertain if I was pressing too far.

He stared at the new dwellings. "This is not the first time Outside has come. The threat of war came from the ocean side long ago. Harold Four-Fingers began bringing Diggers into the army then, as well as using them to collect shards. It worked so well he kept them."

"Was there a war?"

"Yes," he rumbled. "A big one. The Outside could not take the mountain from the sea. Shard weapons were much stronger than their crude metal. Harold threw them back to their boats so fast we did not see their sails on the horizon for many summers. He rewarded the Diggers who had fought by giving them houses, riches, everything. More and more Diggers were brought, and the hoard of shards grew larger. Harold built more ships. We could buy anything we wanted with shards. The difficult part was not to let anyone know where we got them."

I thought of the frowning masks, the secret raids, and the harshness of the Grove. The way of the Spears had been carved deeply and from many years of practice.

My master's cape flickered. "So it started, and has not changed in seventy summers," he said. "How many summers were you a Digger?"

"Eight, or close to that."

"The Spears have been in the mountain for over a hundred summers. This was their first defeat. Their only loss, and still enough are left to rebuild. In time we will be stronger than the old ones were, and we will not be surprised by Outside ever again."

I was so taken by his vision of Grassland, I had not noticed that Tia had walked up behind us to stand even with Marumuk. To my further astonishment he placed his arm around her shoulders. My face reddened and I did not know where to look.

"There is safety here, Coriko," she said, looking up at my master. "And of a kind that we could feel nowhere else."

Marumuk looked beyond us and shouted an order to builders on a rooftop.

I took advantage of his distraction and switched to our Northern tongue. "Slavery and killing, Tia? Is that the safety you are promising us? You know what Pippa says about that."

She glanced down at the ground. "Some things must be done to protect the good of the village. Good and bad are everywhere, Coriko. And here there is a chance for change. I can feel it. It may take a while, longer than Pippa would like, but we can move away from the old ways."

I could tell she was guarding her words, choosing them carefully behind her dark eyes, yet still protecting me.

"The Spears have always had to adjust from time to time," she turned her gaze to Marumuk. "Do you think that in the past a master would ever speak with a thrall as an equal? There is opportunity here, now, for good changes to come. You, Pippa, Thief, and Feelah can help make that happen."

The girl had returned with more bricks. A trickle of blood ran down her leg from a scrape. "One hundred summers, Tia," I answered her. "Yet we still seem to be doing the same things." I looked at Marumuk, who had stepped back to us. "I am honored, master." I saluted him. "We are the chosen."

He saluted back and nodded, seemingly pleased. Tia's face remained cloudy, unreadable. The girl entered a small dwelling down the main road, and I watched Pippa's eyes follow her until the door closed.

Marumuk left us again to speak with a group of soldiers, and Tia began to lead us on the walk back to the mountain. It was an awkward march. I wanted desperately to speak openly with her in front of the others, but with Hammoth present it was impossible. Pippa held my hand tightly from the moment we left the village, as if expecting me to run away or to disappear.

"These are strange times," I whispered when Hammoth moved ahead of us. He scowled at me as he passed.

"Yes," she answered, "even for the Spears. Strange times make for stranger decisions. I understand why Tia is confused."

"How can she turn away from us like this?" I murmured. "She has always been the strongest."

"She has not turned from us. I do not think that her path is leading the best way, but she has never done wrong to us."

I watched the tall brown hair bobbing in front of us, leading us toward the mountain. "Yet," I answered.

The hall of meeting, I learned, was the center of all activity for the girls. Each day they gathered to eat and to learn the language and ways of the Spears. My head was bursting with the newness of it all, and yet there was always more to see. I had never experienced anything like the freedom we were given, except for the early days after our first escape from Grassland. Yet my fear grew and my skin tingled at the thought of what was to come in the night.

"The Spears came a long time ago, in boats with orange sails," Pippa was telling me, pointing at a painting on the far wall of the chamber. The drawing covered most of the rock surface from floor to ceiling, and seemed to be a mixture of lines and small pictures. "The images here," she said, "are where places are. We have drawn things like this many times in our cell, do you remember? It also shows many distant places that the Spears discovered when they traveled in their ships. The country they came from is very far away." She put her finger close to the wall. "Here, I think." Three little soldiers stood with tall shields and helmets that looked something like the frowning masks. Several dwellings had been drawn, but the paint was worn and flaking away. "No one is certain anymore, but they did come from the north, not the south."

"It does not look as if there were many of them in that place," I said.

"No, no. There were many. The pictures do not show all of them. How could you paint everyone? You would have to paint new people when they were born and then scrape them off when they died. It is a picture, Corki.

"Grassland is here." The mountain was clear enough, and it did look much like I had seen it from the boats when we had trained for rowing. "There is also confusion over why they came here," she continued. "The older women say that a vision brought them south. But when I look at the pictures"—she touched a wash of blue and green and I recognized the sea—"I think they were caught in a storm."

I squinted and moved closer. Two ships with orange sails plowed through high waves. The painter had included a dark cloud above them. A white streak—possibly lightning—blazed its way from the sky to the sea.

"It does look like a storm," I agreed.

"Look where the boats were heading. They were going west. Then they hit the storm at mid-sea." She left one hand at the storm and traced the other down to the mountain of Grassland. "And then they end up here in the south." She smiled. "I think Grassland is a mistake."

"A mistake!" I spat out the words.

Thief nudged me. "Maybe the Spears are your people," he snickered.

"No," Feelah said. "Pippa and Coriko were stolen too. Why do you not listen ever?" She smacked the back of his head.

"Old Mira agrees with me." Pippa's smile did not go away. "She remembers our Northern tongue—although not very well, and she will not speak it in front of a male. She is from the old days and does not understand the changes to this place. She will speak to you in Spear."

Feelah giggled, holding her hand over her mouth. "Mira."

"Why is she laughing?" I asked.

Pippa's eyes looked up at the ceiling, then back to me. "Mira is . . . special. She is old, so old that sometimes she does not remember to act properly."

"Where are the old people?" I had never spoken to one before, and I found myself reaching for Pippa's hand.

"They stay in the chambers that have the most light. When Outside came they were brought from the village and hidden in sealed tunnels until Marumuk came for them. Not many made it. Only those who could walk quickly enough from the village were rescued. Mira says it was a terrifying time."

Again my head reeled. It was strange to my ears to hear about the Spears in this way. "I do not want to know about these things." I lowered my voice. "We are leaving anyway. What do they matter?"

"If we are leaving," Pippa glanced quickly around us, "then you should know what is being left behind. And my heart tells me that one day our paths may cross again."

Feelah took us through a tunnel leading to a chamber almost as bright as the hall of meeting. I stopped short the moment we passed through the curtain and saw the people inside. White hair, wrinkled skin, toothless grins. They spoke softly to one another, some sitting, others making their way slowly across the stone floor to a step where water poured into a small drinking pool. There was a peacefulness to the place that made me want to sit and watch without disturbing the old ones.

"Come, Coriko." Feelah tugged at my hand. "These are as safe as shallow water."

None of the old ones stared the way I did and our passing seemed quite normal to them as we made our way to the back of the chamber. Resting on a pallet in a shaft of sunlight, an old woman watched us approach. She greeted Pippa and Feelah warmly, and kissed the sides of their faces.

"Bow," Pippa told me.

Thief and I bent a knee toward the woman. Her voice, when she spoke, came out like the croak of a raven.

"You are Coriko." She gripped my hand and her wrinkled fingers took my palm in a firmer grasp than I expected. She studied my face with eyes that, while faded from their original blue, held me captive with their wisdom. Her skin was so tanned it was difficult to tell which people she came from. "Strong. Good-looking." She glanced at Pippa. "You will have healthy children one day."

Pippa giggled.

"Oooh," Mira gasped before I could respond. "You are a loyal one, are you not? Faithful. Nothing kills you easily, does it? Perhaps not even the Spears."

I jerked my hand away from her.

Pippa laughed and stroked the white hair. "Mira, be nice to him. They are not so good to him in the Grove."

"The Grove, yes," the old woman wheezed. "I should say not." She fixed her eyes back on me. "How was your tree? Comfortable? Could you feel the blood of all the others, seeping through the trunk?"

I took a step back and she cackled. I wanted to hit her.

Feelah spoke this time. "Mira, please be good." With lightning speed the old woman reached out and caught Thief. I reached for my dagger, forgetting that it had been left at the entrance.

"You are Dozt," she croaked.

"Dozt?" I repeated. My hands went back to my sides. "That is your name?"

He nodded.

"It means Thief, does it not?" Mira croaked.

"Your name is Thief even among your own people?" I asked.

"Yah." He looked at me sheepishly.

"Of course it is," I mumbled. "What else would it be."

"You are a leader in your own way, aren't you, my young thief? Both of you boys, I think." The old woman patted his hand. "I wish you could steal my sons back," she sighed. "Marumuk is wise. Good choices. Such pretty men and maids."

I wanted to leave. Were all the old ones as crazy as this?

"Mira," Pippa said softly. "Tell them how long you have been a Spear."

"Awk! A game now, is it? Look at the crone! Listen to the crone!"

"Mira . . ."

"Ninety-two summers."

Thief raised his eyebrows.

Pippa leaned closer to the woman. "What do you remember?"

The woman raised her hand and stroked Pippa's cheek. This time her voice was a bare whisper. "Everything. Everything that has happened."

"Tell us," Pippa said. "Will you come to the map and remember?"

She stood stiffly at my cellmate's coaxing, and I found myself supporting an elbow, tough as leather. Yet she seemed as light as a Onesie. She moved slowly between us, one foot carefully placed at a time. She cocked her head at me a few times and broke into a cackle that I did not like the sound of. It took a long time to return to the hall.

When we reached the map she turned into a different creature. Her hands reached up quickly to touch the rock, and she began tracing the lines that her fingers found there with grace and ease. She pressed her cheek against the cold stone and began to mumble. "Just a young child, I was. So young, with yellow hair reaching to my shoulders. Bouncy, bounce!" She reached for a strand of white hair.

"They took me, of course, and my mother. Father dead, brother dead, of course. No mercy, no, no."

I winced.

"Used to take women back then. What do you call them now?"

"Foursies," Pippa said.

She brought her arms down in front of her face and began to count, touching off the fingers on one hand. "Foursies, yes. Onesie, Twosie, Threesie, Foursie, you see. That was before the rebellion." She turned back to the wall and traced the shape of the beaches.

My ears perked up.

"Some of the women and a few young men tried to escape. No lower cages back then, of course. Didn't last long. Ocean, desert, no place to go. Women were sold. Mother was taken from me in the dead of night. Gone."

"Did any of them get away?" I asked. It had never occurred to me that someone had tried to lead others away before.

She shook a finger at me. "Oh, we don't know that, do we? Never told, never told. Not likely, though. Bones must be long gone now." She thought for a moment, then reached back up to the wall. "Then the children started to come, of course. No more grown-ups. Made them dig just as hard as the rest of us. Dig, dig, dig. All day, diggy-diggy."

My fingers ached just listening to her. "Why did they bring the children?"

She grinned toothlessly. "Little ones can't bite you too badly, can they?" She cackled and shook her head. "After that, lower cages got built. Cleansings started, more children, yes, many more children."

"Tell us about your mate," Pippa encouraged her.

"Ah, yes. Fourteen summers I was. Looked like you." She nodded at Pippa. "Took me from the cages. Gave me to a man, soldier of course. Couldn't speak each other's language, him being from a different place. Didn't matter much. Two children later he was dead—took an arrow through the eye on a raid. Buried him in the yard there along with the first child that didn't make it either." She stopped for a moment, seeming lost in thought, but Pippa said her name and she started talking again. "Got much easier after that. They gave me to another man. A good one. Taught me the Spear language like the other women, and I got treated right enough. They gave me the painting wall when they saw I was clever with my hands." She reached as high as she could and tapped the foot of the mountain just as easily as Pippa could have done it. "That part was hard," she mumbled. "Had to use a standing stone from sunrise to sunset before it was finished. Paint is chipping. Needs work."

"Pippa says," I started slowly, "that the Spears may have come here because of a storm."

Mira nodded. "Could be, could be. Don't know. Too long ago. The oldest ones who told me the stories are long dead, and none of them told the same truth." She looked at Pippa. "But all said something terrible happened at sea and their ships ended up here. Other clues too. The earliest pictures, here and here"—she pointed to a small group of paintings blurred and mottled by age—"these were made before Mira." Her bony hands followed the remains of what looked to be a sail. "See, boats with ruined masts, torn by gales. Yes, pretty Pippa is right, even if no one is left to tell us."

She patted Pippa's head. "Something to dream about, yes? All of us here because of a storm."

Pippa smiled weakly but her words were for me. "If it was a storm that made all this happen, then perhaps something smaller could change it all again." She leaned toward me and whispered, "That is Tia's heart, I think."

Mira reached out her hands to both girls. "I am tired now. Take me back."

We brought her back to the pool where the old people rested. As her hands gripped my arm to steady herself, I felt no need to pull back from her any longer. But I wanted to sit down. After so many summers of being a Digger, I had never expected to understand why. And the answer, as much as it could be known, left a pain in my chest.

"Rest now, Mira." Feelah eased the woman back to a lying position. "I will bring you some food soon." As we moved away from her Feelah whispered, "Bow again."

I gave another low bow and Thief did the same.

Mira cackled and pointed. "Pretty boys! Pretty boys! Where are all my pretty boys?" Her words tumbled after that and I could understand no more. Her head bent to her chest in sleep, her eyes closing even before we turned toward the door.

THIEF STRETCHED TOWARD THE
ceiling. "Ah! I have done nothing for a day and my body
cries to run or wrestle. Careful, Coriko, or I may take
you down to the floor."

We grappled for a moment, testing each others'
balance, then found ourselves tumbling onto the
sleeping cots with a crash. Looking up, Pippa and Feelah
scowled.

"It is time to rest," Feelah scolded. "If we mean to
carry out our plan, there will be little sleep tonight."

Thief nodded and brushed off the dust from his
tunic. "I am not happy with only the four of us going.
Rezah should come, at least. He is a good sword in a
difficult place."

I agreed. "He is trustworthy."

Feelah shook her head. "His mate is not."

"Why?"

"She is happy here. There is no family for her other than Rezah. Of all the girls, she is one I would trust the least with our plans. It is too great a risk to tell Rezah what we are thinking."

To my surprise, Pippa agreed. "It is sad for me to think this way, but Feelah is right. We cannot make others go if they are not willing. I do not want to pit one mate against another. It is best if Rezah does not know."

I thought of my friend's determined face. "I will miss him." No one spoke for a moment.

"What is in Tia's mind?" Thief asked when the quiet became difficult.

"You heard her," I answered. "She knows the secret ways. Marumuk has shown her how to get out."

"And what will we do outside?"

Trusting Tia had been so natural for me that it was hard to think any other way. "We cannot see what she has planned for us. But if she has the right to move about the Spears freely, and has the kind of power that allows her to walk beside Marumuk as his equal, then we can expect much from her—just as we always have."

"Tia will not lead us astray," Feelah whispered.

Thief glanced at Pippa. "Pray that it is so. For if Marumuk should find us, I do not think there will be any mercy handed out."

"We could not even take him with two of us fighting," I added. "Perhaps not even with Rezah."

Pippa took us both in her gaze. "Then I will pray that we are given what we need when the time comes."

For the second time I lay down beside my cellmate. In the cool of the chamber there was little sound other than the odd voice, or the echo of feet in the hall. There was no sign of Tia. After a while Pippa began to tap her hand against the stone.

"What are you thinking?" I whispered, trying to keep my voice lower than Thief's squeaky snore.

"They must come with us, Corki."

"Who?"

"The children that you and Thief stole from the farm."

I groaned. "How?"

"That is what I am thinking about."

I tried to keep my anger in control. "How could we do that? There is already great danger in the few of us escaping, and now you include these others who know nothing. I do not even know if the boy is alive. He may not have survived the Cleansing. I saw only his sister today."

"Can you think of a better way to take the blood off our hands?" she answered. "We cannot change all the wrongs, but we must try to heal the hurts we have caused."

"We do not know where Tia will lead us. We may end up far from the village. What will we do then?"

She thought for a moment. "I will pray that we are given the opportunity to set the evil right. If we cannot do so, then at least we will have tried."

"Oh, Pippa," I grumbled, "you have a lot of praying to do." But I was satisfied. If an opportunity came to save the new Diggers, then it meant we would be in the middle of the Spear village. There was no escape there and I could not think of how a chance would come for us to help them.

I tried to rest, but it felt as if something I had eaten

was trying to win its way back up to my mouth. *Where was Tia?* I listened for her coming, but sleep overtook me, and my body, so used to training every day, gave in to the cool ease of rest.

Someone shook me awake. The chamber was darker than it had been, and I could barely make out Tia's face bending over me. A flint was struck and a candle blazed into light.

"It is time," she whispered. "And there is not much of it."

I gave Pippa a tug.

"Take nothing but what I give you," Tia was saying. "Food is in these two bags. Water you will have to find outside the mountain. Short swords, capes, and daggers are here. And put these on." She handed Spear helmets to Thief and me.

I shuddered as the mask slipped into place. It was the first time I had ever had one on—and in the last place I ever expected to use it. "Will they not track us?" I whispered.

"Not where you are going. You are traveling by boat."

I gripped Thief's arm in excitement. "It is the best way!"

Pippa nodded. "Yes. This time it is good. Tia, do you come with us?"

"For now," came the reply.

"But—"

Tia raised two fingers as a warning. "If we are seen, lower your swords and let me do the speaking. Hide them in your clothes if you can. Should we be challenged by Spears, run. Make your way as quickly as you can down the passage I will show you. It takes you to a long tunnel leading out of the mountain and directly to the ships near the village. This is the escape passage used in time of war. At least five guards watch the boats."

She poked Thief's arm. "Did you hear me? There are five near the boat."

"Yes, Tia. Five." There was no more doubt in his face now.

"Good."

She paused to grip my shoulder. Only then did I see the sweat glistening on her forehead. "Coriko, listen. Only one soldier stands on the middle ship. But what they cannot see in the darkness is a smaller boat, lying ready, tied to that middle ship. You will need to swim out to it, silently, and remain in their shadow until the guard on watch walks to the starboard side of the ship."

She thrust a food bundle toward Thief. "You keep an eye on the watch from the other ships, my Thief. There is danger of being seen by them as well, although less so than by the others. The moon is high. Be as patient as a thief! Go then, and do not look back."

"But you will be with us," Feelah said.

"Let us first get you to safety."

As we moved into the tunnel, I felt the familiar smoothness of my sword's pommel, letting the blade remain out to the side as we had been trained. Thief slipped to the front as always, with Tia, while Pippa and I took the back. Feelah's huge head of hair sent a shadow over us. Few torches lit the passage, but there was easily enough light to see.

Tia took us along a branch I had not been through before, although it seemed to be making for the general direction of the hall of meeting. Behind us, Old Mira would be sleeping, I thought, her wrinkled hands painting her wall in her dreams. What would she think of the "rebellion" happening this night? Under my breath I wished her peace and happiness for the rest of her days. Somehow I knew that if we lived through the night, it would please her to know we had escaped. If only it were now!

Glancing ahead I glimpsed Tia and Thief, their heads close together, stealing us away as they had done so often before. How long had it been since we were crawling over the grasses on our way to the ship? But this time perhaps Tia was not intending to come.

A moment later the two of them froze. As I held on to Pippa I could hear the sound of approaching footsteps. Tall shadows stretched across the stone walls where our own tunnel branched into another.

"Stand tall," Tia whispered fiercely. "Press to the shadows." She dabbed at her brow with her sleeve. "Say nothing."

The footsteps grew louder, and the sound of creaking leather from stiff boots marching in unison reached my ears. As they approached the fork the view became wide enough for all of us to see them. I put a hand out and pressed Pippa farther into the shadow.

Go the other way! Please, go the other way!

Four Spears, all in armor, and with a captain I did not recognize at their head, turned at the fork and straight into our tunnel. I stood as high as I could, holding my arms stiffly to my sides, yet keeping my shoulders in the shadow. We would be lost if they asked us any questions. Our voices would give away our age despite the helmets. Two Red Fists still in training yet wearing frowning masks would raise more suspicion than we could answer for. It was up to Tia now.

The marching line came to a halt.

"Good evening, my lady," I heard a deep voice say.

"Good evening, Captain," Tia's voice called back easily. "I hope it was an uneventful night for you. We go to see the stars from the mountaintop."

"There is much to see, lady," he answered. "We have just come from there. No clouds tonight. The desert is shining."

"My thanks, Captain."

I remembered to salute, holding my breath and praying that they did not look down and see me standing on my toes. The Captain's cape swept over my feet and it was all I could do to hold my balance and not fall over. As the last man passed the line came to a halt again.

"My lady?"

Tia moved as gracefully as she could without running to stand in front of me.

"It is custom to travel with four guards when you go outside of the mountain. And the wild children were spotted again yesterday near the foot where the trees begin. Not a serious danger, but the watch has been more cautious."

Wild children? I stiffened. *Strays!*

Tia dipped her head. "Of course, Captain. Thank you. I will remember next time. I have two of Marumuk's best with me this night and feel more than safe in their company."

The captain nodded curtly. "My lady." Then he spun on his heel and the soldiers moved on down the tunnel.

Tia leaned heavily against the wall, looking as if she were going to be sick.

"Maker help us," Pippa whispered.

I could not find my voice to respond. When Tia regained her breath we moved on with more urgency, no longer walking calmly, but rushing as fast as the light would allow.

Shortly we passed the hall of meeting, although

from a different way than I had seen before. Tia must have taken us on a longer but seldom-used route, to avoid being seen. The room was silent and empty in the dark. No fires blazed on the hearths. As Tia branched away from the hall I thought I heard a voice coming from the opposite end of the great chamber. Tia had clearly heard it too, and she picked up the pace again. She changed tunnels several times until I lost sense of direction completely.

"Do you hear it?" I asked Pippa in a whisper.

"What?"

"There is someone behind us. We are being followed."

"Tell Tia."

I rushed past Pippa and caught up to our Threesie and Thief. "Someone is behind."

Tia mopped her face. "We are almost there."

"They will take you, Tia, if you remain behind," I said.

She did not respond. Instead she led us steadily down a path unlike any of the others we had traveled through so far. The tunnel here was more crudely made. Dust rose from our feet as if no one had walked this way for many days. Only a hundred strides or so later she came to a door, set into the wall of the tunnel.

"At last!" she cried. She pulled out a key from her robe and fumbled with the lock. Her face was ashen even in the dim. When the key turned she stood back and faced us.

"This is where our paths must part. Your prayers have been answered so far, Pippa."

"Come with us, Tia," my cellmate begged.

"I cannot, and there is no time to argue. Go, now. If it is your wish to leave this place, then at least let me grant it while I can."

I stared into her worried eyes but found only tears glistening at the edges.

"Farewell, Coriko," she whispered. "I love you as I did my brother."

"Tia, I—"

"Traitors!" the voice of Hammoth hissed behind me. I spun on my heel, keeping low, with my sword out. Hammoth blocked the way back, his feet spread apart, his dagger glinting. Rezah looked over his shoulder. "Do you see, Rezah? I told you they would run. Was it not wise of us to follow?"

There was nothing I could think of saying. Everything was obvious. My only regret was seeing the disappointment in Rezah's face.

Thief was beside me before I had blinked. Our shoulders pressed against each other as they had a thousand times in the Grove.

"No noise!" Tia begged.

"No killing!" Pippa pleaded.

Thief looked at me and shrugged. "That does not leave us with very much." He beckoned Hammoth with his sword. "Come now, Hammoth!"

"I have known from the beginning you would betray us," Hammoth spat. "Marumuk's little pet and the thief. What a pair, caught like Onesies in a Cleansing cave. Your ruin will be a pleasure for me to watch."

"Rezah," I said quietly, ignoring Hammoth. "You know we had to do this. Would you rather we stayed and killed more people? That is not your heart. You hate this as much as I do—I know it! I wanted you to come, I swear it. You could still, if you want to."

He glanced nervously at Hammoth, then took a look over his shoulder. To my surprise he whispered frantically,

211

"Things are not as they seem. We are not the only ones following you. Run, Coriko!"

"Marumuk!" Hammoth yelled at the top of his voice, sending echoes above our heads and around us.

"Go!" Tia cried. She threw open the door and ducked in. We fled, racing after her as fast as we could, with the sound of stomping feet close behind. Dust rose, filling my nose and forcing me to blink. More tunnels appeared on our left and right but Tia ignored these and ran straight on.

"Faster, Pippa!" I barked. She was doing the best she could in her dress and I wondered suddenly why Tia had not given the girls better wear. But how could we travel openly with the girls dressed as men? Pippa lurched and would have fallen if I had not steadied her.

Tia came to an abrupt stop where the tunnel forked. "Marumuk," she gasped.

The great shape of my master towered above her, and the outline of his sword stretched far past her feet. Not a flicker of movement came from him and if his cape had not swayed in a chance rush of air I might have taken him for a Spear chiseled from stone. His eyes, only a gleam behind the darkened mask, seemed to hold Tia fast.

The tension between them was terrible, like a wave caught between two walls, searching for the weakest to fall. Thief edged to the opposite side of our tunnel, with Feelah clinging to his cape, neither of them taking their eyes off Marumuk. A moment later Hammoth pulled up a few strides behind me. There was no sign of Rezah.

It was Tia who moved first. She stepped purposefully into the junction, allowing the rest of us the freedom, if we dared, to ease behind her to the passage on the right. There was a door with a latch there hanging half open on rusted hinges. Once inside we could shut the others out and run to freedom.

The silence was painful. Tia's breath came in quick heaves but I did not think that it was from running.

"Now is our greatest need." Pippa prayed so quietly I could hardly hear her above my own panting. "Help us now."

Hammoth spoke. "We have them, master."

The big Spear did not even look at him. When he spoke, the shivers down my spine turned to quakes. "Wrath is the greater when trust is broken," he said in a voice like rippling thunder. "And so is pain." Although he could have been speaking to all of us, it was clear his attention was on Tia alone. I could not think of anything she could say or do that might help us at that moment. I stared helplessly at the two of them, shame reddening my cheeks as I looked at Marumuk, only to turn to despair in the face of Tia.

She slowly straightened herself in front of my master and raised her palm in the sign of peace. He did not move or return the sign. I could not see her face, but her words were clear.

"There is nothing ruined here, Marumuk," she said softly, "that cannot be mended." She took one small step toward him.

He held up a hand to stop her. "How is that?"

"I pledge you my life. I pledge you my love. I will remain here as a Spear. In return, I ask that you let these little ones go."

"He is my thrall!" My master jerked his head at me.

But I sensed the change of tone in his voice. He had not expected her to agree to remain behind.

She nodded. "And yet out of your own mouth you

declared him your brother once he left this place. Will you now take back your word?"

"We are brothers by loyalty," he answered. "This is no act of loyalty."

She took another step forward. "You speak of loyalty, Marumuk? Then hear me." She showed an open palm to us. "Their loyalty runs deeper than that of the people of this mountain. By choice, four frightened children are running from an army of trained men. Their loyalty to each other is their honor." She reached him in another step and placed her hand on his powerful arm. "I will be your mate, Marumuk, by choice, by loyalty, and not by command. Please let them go."

"It is not our custom!"

"Then it must become our custom. The ways are changing. We have spoken of this before. All things must begin somewhere; this is a starting place. Listen to me, Marumuk. Will you take us by force or keep me with your heart?" She looked at Pippa, then me.

I stared at her. Her face stood out in the light, her chin determined and her eyes blazing with the confidence of someone becoming a Foursie.

"Let them go, Marumuk. And let us begin the new way."

"It is not so easy as that," he replied, weighing her words, her eyes.

"Not all must be changed in a heartbeat. Only started. Will that not take more courage than raiding a farm of sleeping children?"

"You speak of things you do not yet understand."

She tried a smile. "I speak of things that could be if the might of Marumuk decides it should be so."

He grunted. His bare hands clenched and unclenched. For a horrifying moment I thought he was about to step past her, but his feet rocked back and forth.

"Marumuk . . . ," Tia whispered.

Pippa leaned up to me. "We have been given what we needed." I tore my eyes away from the scene ahead of us. "Tia is our gift," she finished.

When Marumuk still made no response Tia motioned for us to move behind her into the right-hand passage. We walked slowly, holding on to one another, never taking our eyes off the pair in front of us.

Hammoth did not move, his gaze frozen on Marumuk.

As I shuffled to get by them, Marumuk raised a long finger and pointed at me. "Life for life, Coriko."

In my heart I remembered his eyes as the farmer had raised the sword above my master's head. "Life for life," I repeated.

"Remember me," Tia whispered as we passed.

"Always," Pippa answered.

For the last few steps it did not seem possible that the impossible was happening. But Pippa was right: we had been given what we needed. None of us would ever forget Tia. I closed the door on Hammoth and my master, seeing Tia's pretty face for the last time before her path was chosen forever.

14

WE PLUNGED INTO DARKNESS.
No torches lit the passage and we were forced to use our hands along the tunnel sides to find our way.

"Hurry, hurry!" Thief urged.

"Why? We are safe now."

"I did not hear Marumuk agree to anything, did you?" he replied.

I picked up my pace, forcing Pippa to move faster.

"How far will the tunnel go before we come out from the mountain?" Feelah whispered. "I do not like the darkness."

My heart agreed. Too long had we lived in the tunnels as slaves—I longed to smell the ocean. I kept waiting for sounds behind us, or for light to suddenly burst from some hidden hole, and to see Marumuk's hands leaning out to crush us.

"Courage, Feelah," Pippa answered. "For once, we are going the right way." There was a joy to her voice, so different from the first time we had tried to leave Grassland. I took hope from it.

"Did you hear what the captain said about the wild children?" I asked Pippa.

"Yes. Strays."

"Why has Marumuk not crushed them, I wonder?"

"They are no threat to armed Spears," Thief said. "They would have to be hunted. The work is better spent on rebuilding the village."

Pippa spoke up. "It will not be long, I think, before Marumuk turns his eyes to the Strays. They will not be able to hide from the Spears. May Tia's words turn him to mercy."

"Some well-placed arrows would do the work well," I mumbled. "Filthy Strays." It seemed good to me that Marumuk would deal with them soon. I would never forgive them for taking Bran. He would still have been with us, and so would Tia, if it had not been for the Strays.

The passage continued to descend for some time. My sword kept getting tangled whenever I got too close to Pippa, so I was forced to keep one hand on the hilt to angle it away from my body. From time to time the scabbard would scrape along the tunnel wall, and the sound of it set my heart pounding.

Feelah spoke a while later but I did not understand the words.

"The path is no longer going down," Pippa explained in our own language. "It is straight."

"Straight but long. Does this have an end?" I muttered.

"Peace, Corki."

"It should not be far to swim to the boats," Thief was saying.

"We have something to do at the village first," Pippa said.

I cringed. Ever since Tia had mentioned that our path would take us close to the ruins, I had been hoping that Pippa had not noticed. It was not so.

Thief stopped walking, and even in the darkness I could sense the question on his face as he tried to find Pippa. "What purpose do we have at the village?"

"To rescue the children stolen from the farm."

"Madness," he replied. "We are fleeing from the Spears, only to run back into the heart of their new dwellings? You are asking too much, Pippa. Why can you never be satisfied? Does Coriko know of this thinking?"

"Yes," I mumbled.

In the darkness and dust of the tunnel I heard Pippa planting her feet. "Even if we escape tonight from this mountain, do you think that the blood on our hands will wipe off so easily? Do you not think of them, Thief, the children you stole?"

There was silence.

"I do not think of them as much as you," he finally answered. "But yes, I think about them."

Feelah spoke quietly. "I think of them every moment my eyes are open," she said to him. "If I had not been so frightened with Marumuk chasing us all about the place, I would have thought more of them. I am with Pippa. If there is something for us to do, then we should do it."

Thief groaned. "We are not out of the mountain yet and already you are speaking of rescues."

"My Thief will help and so will I," Feelah announced.

"Good." Pippa stamped her foot.

Thief found me and knocked the front of my helmet with his own. "You are an idiot," he whispered.

"You too."

"How will we get them out?" Feelah asked. "We saw all the soldiers there today."

"Then it must be soldiers who get them out," Pippa said. "Perhaps for one time only I will be happy to see you two dressed in Spear armor." She might have been grinning, but I did not like the thought of entering that village again for any reason.

"Madness," Thief grumbled again. But he turned away from me and took the front of our tiny line. From time to time we stopped to listen for anyone following, but the silence was heavy both in front and behind. Echoes shuffled around us as we moved forward again, sending frightening images of marching feet to my racing thoughts.

"I can hear the sea!" Thief croaked a while later. We stopped.

"There is light ahead," Feelah whispered. "Not torches, though. Stars!"

"I can feel the wind," Pippa said. "And look, there is no wall on our left."

I put my hand out and discovered she was right. The rock tunnel had disappeared, to be replaced by the blackness of thick woods. So quickly had we come to the end that I looked back to find the tunnel mouth.

"The path goes on," Thief said. "Through the woods. The village will lie in that direction."

Above us the mountain towered in moonlight, its balding head reaching for the blackness of the sky. After the pitch darkness of the tunnel, the trail ahead seemed fairly easy to follow. My feet felt the comfort of the forest floor and I sighed at the protection the woods offered. Marumuk was far behind us, and I found strength in the night air.

"Swords out, Coriko," my friend reminded me. "We do not know how far the watch will be set."

We picked our way with the ocean on our left, allowing the stars to show us the direction. It could not be far, for Tia had said that the boats would be found near the village. It was only a matter of keeping from being seen. And praying that Tia was able to keep Marumuk from sounding the alarm.

Thief suddenly froze. "Someone is ahead."

"I hear nothing," I answered. My sword had found its way higher, thrusting out in front of my chest.

"They are all around us," he whispered.

"Where?"

Thief rested his back against mine and we pulled the girls to our sides. And then the foul smell came—creeping, riding on the breeze from the sea.

"Strays," Feelah said.

"Can we never be rid of trouble?" I hissed. "How many?"

"All of them, I think." Pippa wrinkled her nose.

"There is strength in stone," Thief said.

"And two are better than one," I finished.

A snarl erupted from the bush and three wild forms leaped onto the path from either side of the trail. The first fell to the ground without a sound, clutching his head where I had smacked him with the side of my sword.

"Please, no killing, Corki!" Pippa cried.

"Be quiet, Pippa!" I herded her closer to Feelah, then thrust again as another came at us. I struck resolutely, without mercy, yet avoiding the edge of my blade. He spun dizzily to the nearest tree and fell over.

Six or seven charged at once from many directions. I could hear Thief grunting as he laid forth stroke after stroke on unprotected heads. A robe suddenly tore and I could feel Pippa being pulled away. I kicked hard into a chest and she fell down at my feet. My dagger was out now as well, and I was ready to spill blood. Much of it.

Just as my arms began to tire I heard the familiar twang of an arrow being loosed, and a Stray fell headlong before he reached me. More arrows were loosed and the Strays fell back, running wildly into the brush. My chest heaving, I spun to look for the latest attacker.

Two Spears stepped from the trees. One of them spoke. "All is well?"

I glanced at Thief, who was pulling himself free from a Stray lying limp at his ankles. The girls stared from the Spears to the woods.

"All is well." The words flowed from my mouth by habit. Marumuk had indeed worked quickly. But the sentry's next words made me straighten.

"Why are you here?" His bow was still at ready, but it

was aimed toward the woods. His partner turned from us to watch the trees behind.

Thief had raised himself to a sitting position, his body covering the Stray's face. He nodded at the two girls and pitched his voice lower. "Marumuk sends these two on their way to the village."

"For what purpose?"

I joined in, coughing first to rough up my voice. I could only hope that the cover of darkness would be our friend. "Our orders were to take these two to the village. They are servants of the Lady Tia." I coughed again. "There will be a visit tomorrow. The lady will be here, and needs a place made ready."

"The last report had the wild ones on the far side of the mountain," Thief added. "This was deemed the best way."

The soldier turned his bow to a sound in the wood. "We have had no news of this." Another crash made him turn again. "But it is best to come with us now. I have never seen the wild ones so close before, or in such numbers. We will show you the way, then come back to make certain none have returned. Hurry." He glanced down at the Stray in Thief's grasp.

"What will you do with him?"

"This one, we will take," Thief said. "Marumuk will have words for him, I am sure." He glanced at me. "Help me carry him."

My eyebrows rose high beneath the helmet.

"Hurry then," the Spear commanded. "It is not far."

Grabbing the boy by the shoulders, Thief and I dragged the Stray after the girls, my thoughts racing at the turn of our plans. I did not dare to catch Pippa's frightened gaze, and I forced myself to try to think clearly. I grunted with the weight. It was a sturdy boy we carried. He would make a good Spear in time. I hardly noticed his groans as I wondered how we would make a break for the ships before the night was over.

More sentries greeted us before long, their marching footsteps falling in with us as we made for the looming gates of the village. There were no lights, as the Spears had long made certain that nothing would attract ships to these shores. Once inside the gates, the sentry who led us paused.

"There is lodging in the new residences along the central road," he pointed. "It is still a crude warrior's

227

place and not much comfort for the women. I cannot understand why they would come here."

"The lady is anxious to have a home," Pippa said honestly.

It was the first time either girl had spoken, and I marveled at her courage. I hoisted the Stray a little higher. "Then there will be much for them to do if the lady comes in the morning," I said.

The soldier shrugged. "Strange times."

"Where does this one go?" Thief tugged at our captive.

"Holding cell with the Onesies."

My friend's eyes glimmered beneath his helmet.

"I am afraid it is close to the residences"—the sentry glanced at the girls—"but with your mistress coming soon, I am sure that will change." He looked at me. "Can you put him in? We should not be long from the woods with these vermin running about. They are like ship rats—they steal anything. At least we made a dent in their numbers this night."

It did not take us long to find the Onesies. It was the only dwelling with a solid door and no windows. A latch and hook kept anyone from leaving.

"I will praise you for your wisdom later," I whispered to Thief in the silent road. "I thought at first that your thinking was bent for dragging a Stray along."

Thief surprised me by gently letting our burden down outside the door. "It is not a Stray," he said with a chuckle.

I leaned down in the moonlight to look.

"Bran."

15

I FELL TO MY KNEES AND TOOK hold of the shaggy-headed boy. "Bran!" I whispered with as much joy as I could allow myself. His eyes remained closed. "Stupid Onesie!" I said happily. "Even when we finally find you after all these dangers, you are sleeping!"

"Is he harmed?" Pippa asked.

"I hit him pretty hard," Thief admitted. "I did not know it was him until the arrows started. It is good fortune I did not strike him with my dagger."

Pippa smiled quickly. "It was not fortune that put him with us again."

"Come," Feelah hissed. "Let us do what we must."

I looked down the road at the retreating Spears, then

up at the residences. Bran gave a groan and opened an eye.

"Pippa?" he stared over my shoulder.

She gripped my arm as she leaned down to him. "Peace! Be quiet, Bran. We are trying to get away. All of us . . . almost all of us."

His eyes opened fully and he took us in.

"Bran," I whispered. "It is Coriko. Here is Thief and Feelah."

He stared at the helmet. "What are you doing in that thing, and where is Tia?"

I looked at Pippa.

"She is safe, Bran," my cellmate said. "Listen to me! We are still in great danger here. You must be quiet and get up if you can. If all goes well, we can answer questions later."

He shook his head slowly, rubbing a growing bump on his forehead.

Pippa took charge. "Let me go in to the children," she told us. "Feelah must come too. When they are out we will have to find another way out of the village. Show your faces to them as they step from the door."

"There is only one gate." Thief looked over his shoulder. "How else can we get out? We cannot scale that wall."

"Not with all these children," I agreed.

"What did he say?" Bran asked me, bewildered. When I told him, he spoke again, his words sounding clearer this time. "There is a hole in the wall. That way." He pointed to the far end of the village. Then he grinned. "We have to watch from somewhere. You Spears are hard to steal from."

I undid the latch and let Pippa slip inside. Feelah went in a moment later. Soon we could hear stirring and the sound of children's voices.

"Keep them silent," I muttered under my breath. The night was growing deeper, as were my fears. It was strange to be standing outside the dwelling this time, waiting impatiently while my mate stole the children. At least we were stealing them back.

Thief watched the road and Bran kept a close eye on the gate. I glanced at him from time to time, shaking my head that he was with us. Without turning I risked a whisper. "How are you still alive?"

He stiffened, but did not take his gaze from the gate. "I floated to shore among all the baskets and bundles as everyone was fleeing. I had no strength and lay like a dead man until it was light. Not even the Spears touched me on their way to get at you in the boat. There was a lot of blood on me and they thought I was dead. When I finally got up, everyone had left. There was no place for me to go, so I went back to the stream-trees. I knew it was only a matter of time before the Strays found me, so I ripped up my clothes and blended in among them the first chance I found."

I could not stop a smile.

He continued. "I looked as filthy as they did, and must have smelled as bad too. Everyone was in confusion because of the Spears returning."

He was about to say more when the door suddenly nudged against my arm. Feelah stepped out first. I raised my helmet so that my face peered out from behind the frowning mask. The children came out quickly, fearfully staring up into the shadows of my face before following after Feelah. Bran went to join her. The girl I had taken from the farm was one of the last to leave. She gasped when she saw me, but Pippa spoke quietly to her and held her hand tightly.

Madness, I thought as I stared over the heads of our winding line. Fourteen. All of them had made it through the First Cleansing—unless they never had been taken to the lower cells in the first place.

Thief had moved to the front of the line, although I could see it was Bran who was really doing the directing. There was not much hope of another ruse, however, on the open street. Our greatest chance was to get into the darkness of the unfinished dwellings as soon as possible and pray that no sentries found us.

Bran did not wait long to move into shadow. Thief turned sharply before we had even reached the residences, and within strides we were covered by the blackness of tall walls and wooden roofs. I picked my way through bricks and stones until I reached my friends. Pippa was doing her best to keep the children quiet, although she hardly had to remind them that being found could only result in one thing.

"Sentry," Thief hissed, pointing ahead.

The soldier was cleverly placed, barely noticeable

among the boards and planks laid out for the next day's work. His spear moved slightly as he shifted his position.

Thief lifted his hand, then made a circle with his finger. *Go around.*

I shook my head. There was no choice. I was about to tell Pippa about the sentry when one of the children stumbled and cried out. There was a rumble as a brick rolled over, and the sentry suddenly turned in our direction.

"This way!" Bran took off before I could lay a hand on him. Behind me, the children began to scatter. I grabbed hold of the nearest one around the back of the neck.

"Pippa, this way!" I whispered frantically.

She and Feelah followed me, each holding two children by the hand. I waited until they had caught up, threw the child I was holding toward Pippa, then set out after Thief. He was already racing toward the sentry.

I watched him approach the guard, hailing him with an open palm. I slowed my speed, and slunk to the side of the new dwelling, desperately trying not to trip in the darkness.

"It was a Onesie," Thief was saying. "Must have broken out somehow."

The guard was facing my friend, unaware of what was behind him.

"Who are you?" the guard growled, starting forward.

I took him below the knees, crunching his legs together as we had been taught, so that he could not regain his balance. Once he was on the ground, Thief cut the Spear's helmet strap before he could raise his arms. Flipping his frowning mask off, I struck his head with the back of my dagger.

"Corki!" I heard Pippa's quiet whisper. "This way."

Bran led us to the great wall surrounding the village. I found myself leaning against it for support. I kept sucking in air and glancing wildly about for more sentries. Besides my nervousness there was also a strange rush of confidence flowing through me that made me want to shout. Thief and I had just taken down a grown Spear. The power of it made me giddy.

"What happened back there?" Pippa whispered. Five children clustered around us.

"Nothing."

The hole in the wall was hardly big enough for us to get through. Thief and I had to hand our helmets out first before we could slip through ourselves.

"I know my way around here," Bran said as we huddled together outside the wall. "We have been here many times at night. Where are we going?"

"The beach."

"Only five?" Pippa stared at the children's faces around her. "There are only five here?"

Feelah spoke softly. "There is only one path to take now. We have done what we can. Even you know that."

Pippa stared at the hole we had just escaped through, then nodded. She hugged the nearest child.

"There are ships waiting in the harbor," I told Bran.

"I saw them. Another pulled up this morning."

"We have a small boat waiting for us, tied to the middle ship."

He nodded. "Where is Tia?"

I flipped my helmet off. "She is with the Spears."

Starlight flickered in his eyes.

"She is with the Spears by choice."

He looked to Pippa, completely confused. She took one of the little ones standing beside her and turned the child so that she faced Bran.

"She chose to stay so that none of these would ever come to harm again."

"How is that possible?"

"She will wed the master of the Spears."

Poor Bran swung his gaze back to me. "Then I will go to her."

I shook my head. "She does not have power yet. It will take time. You would not make it alive to the place where she is. And then you really would be dead to her. Come with us, Bran. It is what your sister would want."

"The wait is not good," Thief growled impatiently.

"We have to go, Bran. There is no time for grief now. Be glad that your sister is alive. You may yet see her one day." He did not say another word but squeezed past me to take the lead into the woods.

Three ships lay in the harbor, exactly as Tia had told us. The tall masts rode the gentle swells easily. We approached the beach as we had so many days ago, creeping through the grass until we reached the sand.

"Can these little ones swim?" Thief asked me.

"I hope so."

The girl I had stolen from the farm held tightly to her brother's hand. She glanced at me from time to time, but for the most part stayed as near to Pippa as she could. It was hard to blame her. At least her confusion was gone. It was clear that she wanted to be as far away from the Spears as we did.

Thief suggested that we take the Spear equipment with us until we reached farther shores, but I hated him for it at that moment. It was difficult trying to swim with a helmet on. The heavy metal pressed my head to the water, and I constantly snuffed splashes up my nose. My cape was rolled in a tight ball and I pushed it into each new swell, grumbling with every effort. To make things worse, one of the Onesies kept reaching out for me until eventually I had to tow her with my rolled-up cape.

Pippa and Feelah swam on their backs, trailing our swords on their stomachs. Bran held the food bag. The other four kept up as best they could, all of them terrified. The crash of the waves on the beach covered any sounds we were making, and I was grateful as well for the wind whistling through the rigging of the boats.

Feelah reached the rowboat before the rest of us. She hoisted herself in, then stretched her arms out to help us as we approached. It seemed a thousand summers before all of us lay sputtering and heaving to catch our breath on the wet planks of the boat. And a thousand summers more for our strength to return—as anxious as I was to leave, I knew we could not row without strength.

"Nothing moves," I whispered. From the stern I could see no watchers, although there were no lights shining to show them.

"It is time." Thief pulled his knife and turned to the anchoring line to cut our boat free. "Help me, Coriko." It was too thick for our daggers, and it was well we had brought our swords. Together we worried at the knots until our hands bled.

"It is too thick."

Pippa took the dagger from my belt. Gripping the line, she placed her legs firmly around the rope and began to climb. With raider speed Thief and I slipped the oars into place and brought the boat under her, pulling up to the ship's side. Feelah reached up and caught Pippa's feet, holding her steady as she worked at the rope.

My eyes froze on the Spear standing guard on the ship to our port side. His own boat was riding a wave, and in that moment its bow rose into the circle of the moon, lighting his frowning mask for the skies to see. He faced the open ocean, looking ceaselessly for unseen enemies. My chin sank to my chest in relief. Our boat rocked gently and I lifted my head to watch Feelah deliver Pippa to her feet once again. We were free.

"Now we must wait for the guards to change sides," Thief whispered.

It was hard work keeping our small boat in the shadow of the ship with our tie lost. It was even harder to keep the oars quiet. Finally, when my muscles ached so badly I thought I could not take another stroke, Pippa waved. Heavy footsteps walked above us as the guard moved from the port to the starboard side. Bran gave a mighty push off the mother ship and the ten of us slipped, for the first time, through the shadow of night, away from the mountain of the Spears.

Our oars dipped and caught in the waves, with only the odd spray breaking over the sides. We made for the nearest coast, the reaching arm of the mountain, to hide behind its stony curtain.

I rowed as I had never rowed before, feeling Thief's strong strokes pulling evenly with my own. In front of me Pippa sat with the children, catching my eye once in a while and smiling. Her hair blew in the wind, whisking strand after strand around her pretty cheeks. I rowed even harder.

Once out of sight of the ships we lifted the small sail lying at the bottom of our boat. It caught, billowed, then filled to fullness with a snap. Pippa started to cry with joy. Feelah hugged her wet face, laughing. Thief still had his helmet on and, as if suddenly remembering, pulled it off and dropped it with a thud to the boards below. His grin fit him better than a mask.

"I will miss my sister." Bran stared over my shoulder.

With the tiller firmly in my grasp I kept my eyes set on the open sea.

"She is happy, I think," I answered. "Her decision not only saved us, but has given her purpose as well."

"Happy?" He sounded hollow and hopeless. "What will my mother and father say?"

"We are hardly out from the shadow of the mountain and you are talking as if we sat for food at your father's table," I said.

Pippa leaned against Bran's shoulder. "My heart tells me we will see her again. Perhaps your parents will too."

He only sighed.

"You're a stupid Onesie," I said.

My own hair blew freely and whipped into my eyes. Pippa would braid it when the sun found our boat in the morning. There was plenty of time for that now, plenty of time for everything, far from Grassland's shores.

ABOUT THE AUTHOR

David Ward was born in Montreal, Quebec, and grew up in the city of Vancouver beside the mountains and ocean. He was an elementary school teacher for eleven years before completing his master's degree. David is currently a writer and university instructor in children's literature. He lives in Portland, Oregon, with his wife and three children. This is the second book in a trilogy of Grassland adventures. Visit him online at www.davidward.ca.

THIS BOOK WAS ART DIRECTED

and designed by Chad W. Beckerman. The text is set in 12-point Adobe Garamond, a typeface that is based on those created in the sixteenth century by Claude Garamond. Garamond modeled his typefaces on ones created by Venetian printers at the end of the fifteenth century. The modern version used in this book was designed by Robert Slimbach, who studied Garamond's historic typefaces at the Plantin-Moretus Museum in Antwerp, Belgium. The display type is Charlemagne.

SNEAK PEEK FROM

BOOK THREE OF

THE GRASSLAND TRILOGY

BEYOND THE MASK

I

THE RAIDERS CAME ON HORSE-
back. No fewer than twenty mounts trotted through
the sparse trees and meadow, making their way to
the unsuspecting village below. All were seasoned
warriors—their war-cloaks were stained by water and
sun, blood and time, and blended with the dark woods
on either side of them. There was not a common helmet
on their heads, but rather a foul collection taken from
the fallen in past battles. It was the way of a reckless,
merciless army. It was the way of Outside.

"We come too late," Thief whispered. "This will be
a slaughter. We should leave." He held a hand in front

of his mouth to hide his cloudy breath. It was cold in this land. Colder than Pippa had said.

I stuffed my numb hands deep into my cloak. Thief's words rang ominously, but I didn't answer. Pippa had brought us here without disaster, and I would not go against her wishes so quickly. Not after coming so far. So long.

Her eyes watched the rough column of soldiers. "There is time enough to warn the village," she said.

I gauged the distance between the first horses and the final slope. Dawn's pale light breaking across the water, coupled with a half moon, lit the way for the riders. "Not much time, Pippa. There are ten of us, on foot. If we hurry we might be able to warn the villagers enough that they can defend themselves. But not to escape. There is little place to hide down there from men on horseback." Dark green trees, taller than any we had seen in Grassland, kept us hidden. A fog rolled in from the sea and rested above the near fields like hearth smoke. I pursed my lips. It was a cold place, with dampness everywhere, and yet alive with greenness and fresh earth. I was thankful for the warm cloaks we had found in the boat that had carried us here.

Pippa followed my gaze. The village was small. No more than ten small dwellings, nestled between the mountains and the sea. The homes clustered around a central path, with trees on either side hedging the village like cupped hands around a bowl. There were farms as well, but these were cleverly cut into the steep sides of the mountains like steps, difficult to get to, and spaced large distances apart. The easiest catch was the village, where there was food, water, and whatever other spoils the raiders could drag away with them.

I lifted Pippa's chin. "Do you wish us to risk everything for a village you are not even certain is your own?"

Her eyes, so green, stared back with the confidence of a soldier. "Do you need to ask?"

A warm brown hand rested on my shoulder and

Feelah knelt beside us. "Coriko. Why do we all have to go? Why not just two? The little ones do not need to see another battle. You and my Thief go. Yell and make noise, then run for the woods. You will be gone before the raiders arrive, and everyone will be up with whatever weapons they have." She shrugged. "Then at least we have done what we can."

Pippa raised her eyebrows. Thief nodded. I turned my attention to where Bran watched over the little ones. It was difficult for him not to be discussing plans. He was even getting better at speaking the language that united the rest of us: the language of warriors and slaves, the language of the Spears who had so long held us in thrall. How long ago that was. Spring and summer had passed. Winter, in all its bitterness, had kept us from exploring any farther north, and our days were spent seeking warmth.

For more than three seasons we had been in this country, searching in vain for the village that Pippa had been taken from when the Spears stole her and brought her to Grassland. Pippa was constantly remembering more: names of places, lakes, mountains. But they were like a map drawn by a child—confused and with no understanding of distance.

I looked at my companions. We were a tired, ragged-looking company. Our clothes, soaked by the sea, bleached by the sun, and beaten by the winter, were ill-fitting at best. The boat we had taken from Grassland seemed to grow smaller each day. I despised even looking at it anymore.

Bran watched me with a furrowed brow. I signaled, *Come*. Keeping low, he scrambled to my side. "What will we do?" He used the Northern tongue—a language, I realized, that the people sleeping in the village below might use.

"Feelah says two go down to warn the village. The rest stay here. I doubt the raiders will enter the woods, so you should be safe here. There is a direct path through the meadow to the fjord."

His eyes narrowed. "You mean three of us go down."

I grunted. "If one of the little ones cries, or scouts

are sent to the trees, we need you to be here. You must take them into thicker woods or back into the boat. And you have no skill with a sword yet. You would just as likely cut me down as one of the raiders!"

Pippa interrupted us. "This is my village. At least, with all my heart I believe it is. Do you see that last building? The one closest to the sea?"

I nodded. "Past the village, beyond the rise?"

"Yes. I have seen it before—I am sure of it." She took a deep breath. "Feelah's words are good. Not all should be in danger because of me. Coriko and I must go."

"I do not like it," Thief growled. "We have been in danger before. And this is not the first village we thought was Pippa's. This is no different than any others. Coriko and I should go. There may be fighting."

Pippa slapped the ground. "This is the village. I know it!"

Thief and I exchanged glances. I could not remember the number of times we had crawled through fields or crept into towns all along this coast, only to discover that we had not found Pippa's home. And we could not ask where it was, since her memory of the name had left her. It was a name she knew she would remember if she heard it, but that was no help to us now.

When the number of our days since leaving Grassland passed one hundred and fifty, I stopped hoping in names, and trusted only in letting Pippa see as many villages as we could. She would have to see it, and yet there seemed no end of little towns along this coast. Summer had turned to fall and then winter, and still we had not found it.